ROBERT LOUIS STEVENSON'S

TREASURE ISLAND

A GRAPHIC NOVEL

BY WIM COLEMAN,
PAT PERRIN, &
GREG REBIS

STONE ARCH BOOKS
A CAPSTONE IMPRINT

Graphic Revolve is published by Stone Arch Books
A Capstone Imprint
1710 Roe Crest Drive, North Mankato, Minnesota 56003
www.capstonepub.com

Cataloging-in-Publication Data is available at the Library of Congress website.
Hardcover ISBN: 978-1-4965-0008-3
Paperback ISBN: 978-1-4965-0027-4

Summary: Young Jim Hawkins discovers an old treasure map and sets out on a harrowing voyage to a faraway island. The violent sea is just the first of many obstacles, as Jim soon learns there are dangerous men seeking the same treasure.

Common Core back matter written by Dr. Katie Monnin.

Designer: Bob Lentz
Assistant Designer: Peggie Carley
Editor: Donald Lemke
Assistant Editor: Sean Tulien
Creative Director: Heather Kindseth
Editorial Director: Michael Dahl
Publisher: Ashley C. Andersen Zantop

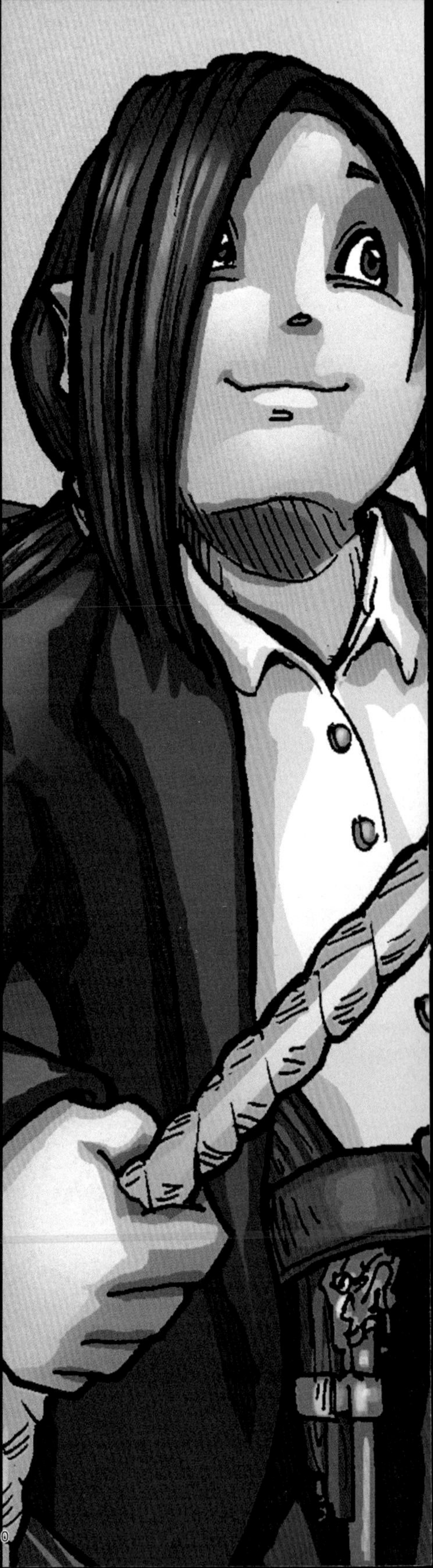

Printed in the United States 4300

TABLE OF CONTENTS

ABOUT SAILING SHIPS

In the 1700s, the world was filled with sailing ships. People crossed the oceans, transported goods, and explored new lands using wind power and strong ocean currents. In seaside towns, ships were loaded along the wharves, or docks. A captain called his ship "shipshape" or "seaworthy" if it was ready to go to sea. And when the captain yelled "all hands on deck," the crew boarded, ready to set sail.

Each person on a ship had their own special job to do. Cabin boys, hoping to learn more about sailing, served the captain. The captain steered the ship by turning the ship's tiller. Crew members would lift and lower the heavy sails. To keep the ship in one place, the crew would drop an anchor. If a ship went adrift, or off course, the crew sometimes stopped the ship by breaching it, or sailing it onto land. The life of a sailor was hard, and many crew members never made it back home alive.

Ships often traveled on the "high seas," or waters that were not owned by any country. Life on the high seas was filled with dangers. A ship could sink in a storm or become shipwrecked. Crews could be stranded on strange islands or coastlines. Pirates could attack. To show they were in command of a ship, pirates would "raise the Jolly Roger" or hang a black flag that had a skull and crossbones on it, from a high mast.

CAST OF CHARACTERS

Jim Hawkins

Dr. Livesey

Ben Gunn

Billy Bones

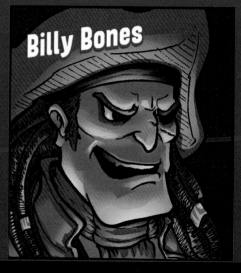

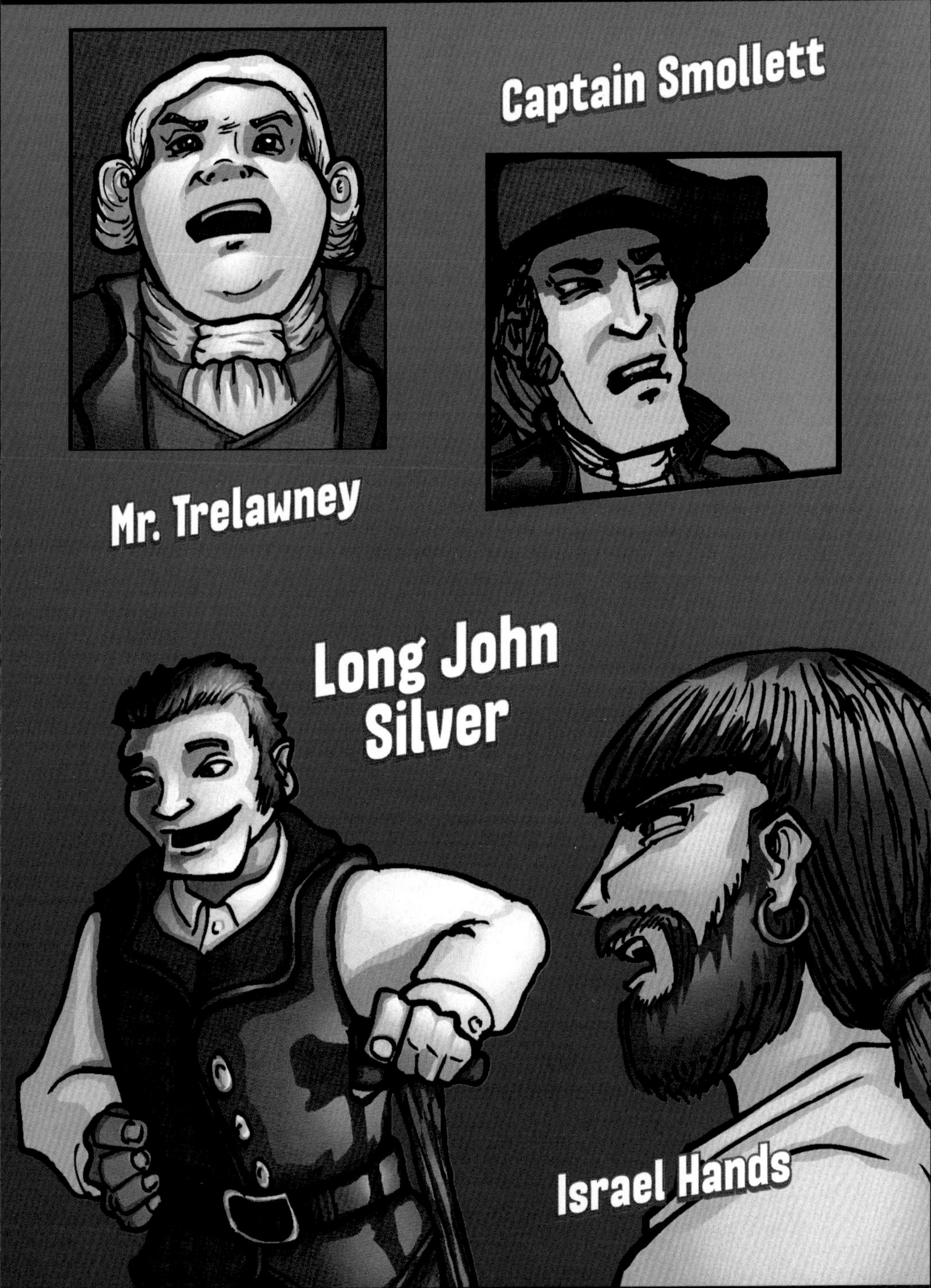
Captain Smollett
Mr. Trelawney
Long John Silver
Israel Hands

CHAPTER 1 The Old Sea Captain

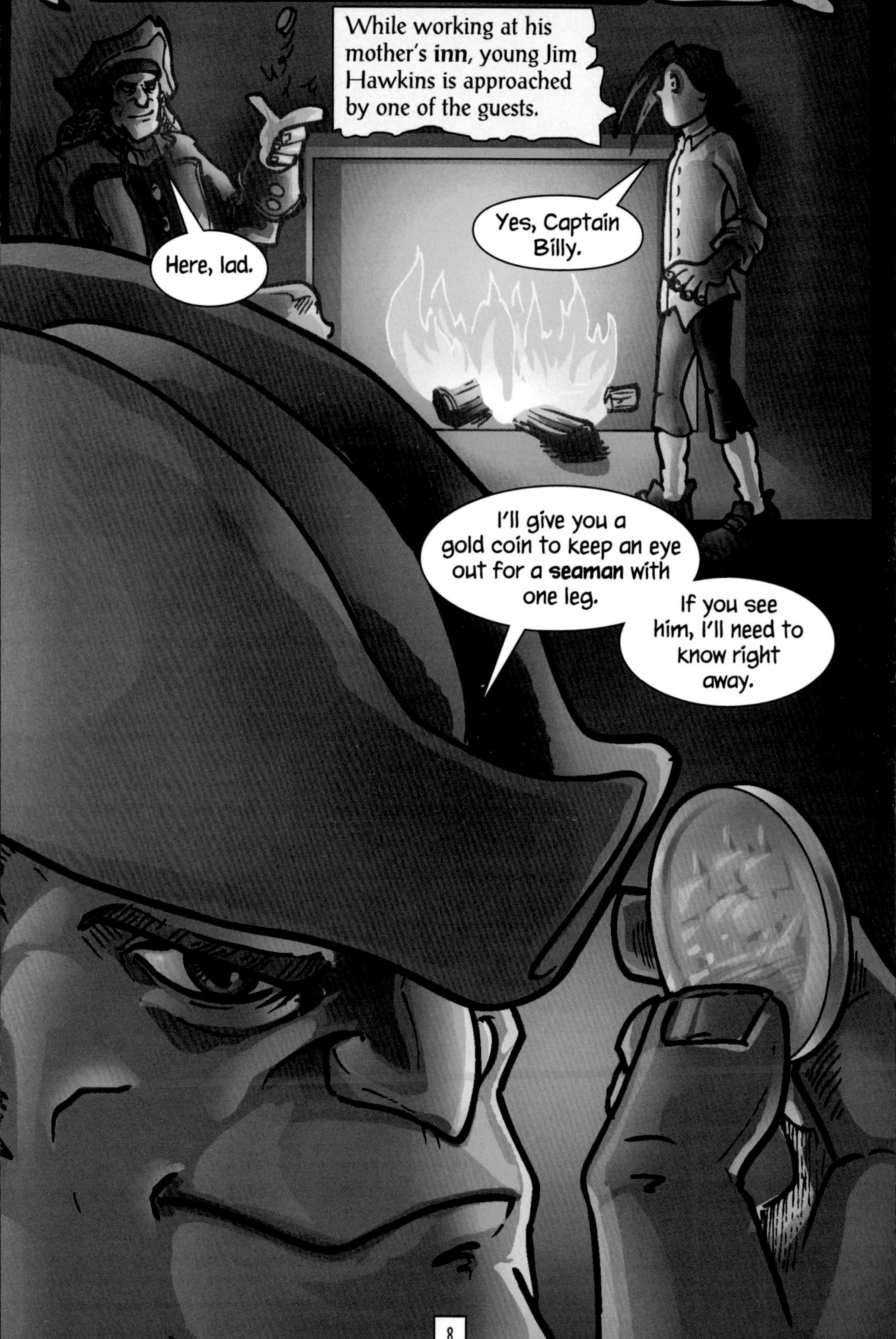
While working at his mother's inn, young Jim Hawkins is approached by one of the guests.
Here, lad.
Yes, Captain Billy.
I'll give you a gold coin to keep an eye out for a seaman with one leg.
If you see him, I'll need to know right away.

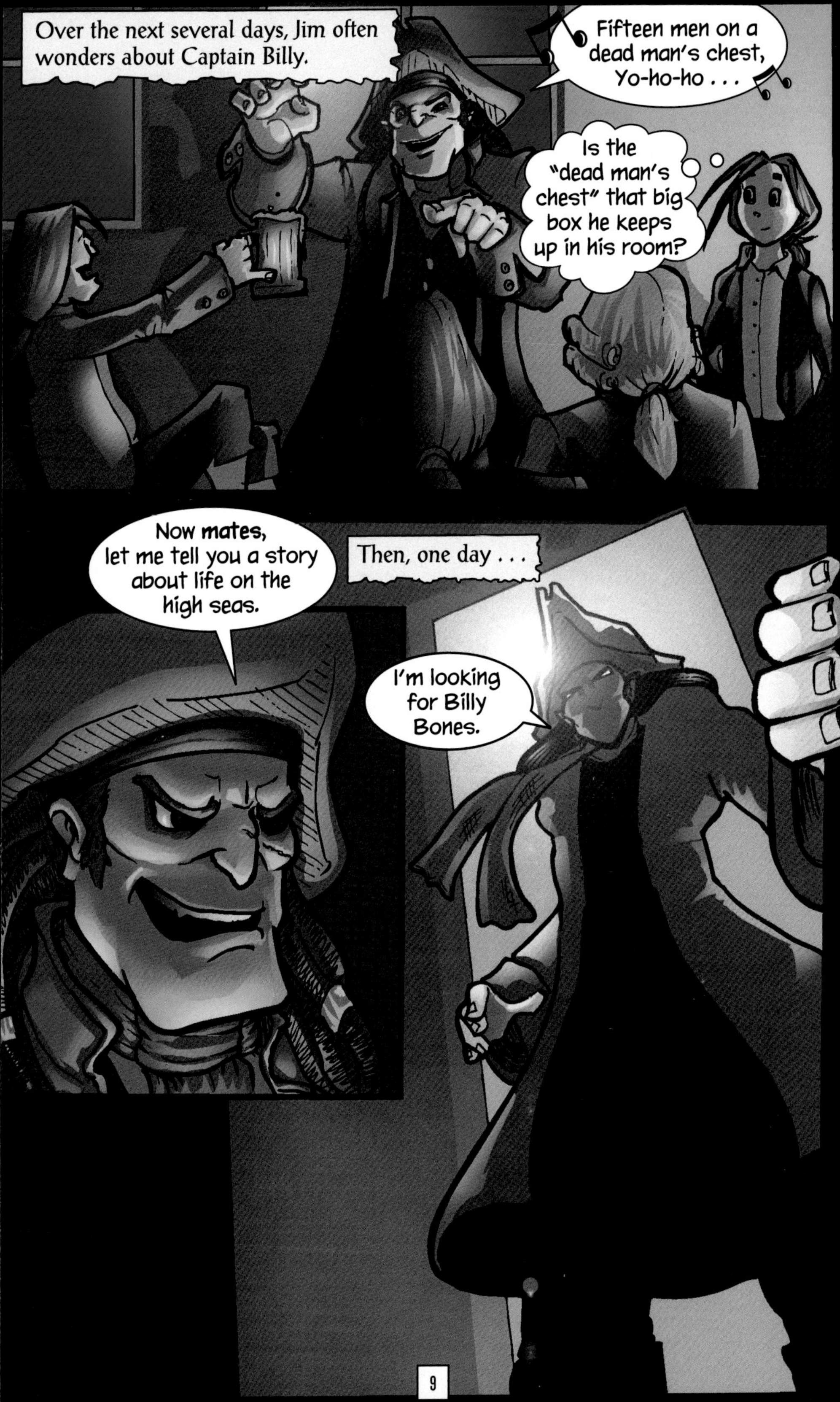
Over the next several days, Jim often wonders about Captain Billy.
Fifteen men on a dead man's chest, Yo-ho-ho . . .
Is the "dead man's chest" that big box he keeps up in his room?
Now mates, let me tell you a story about life on the high seas.
Then, one day . . .
I'm looking for Billy Bones.

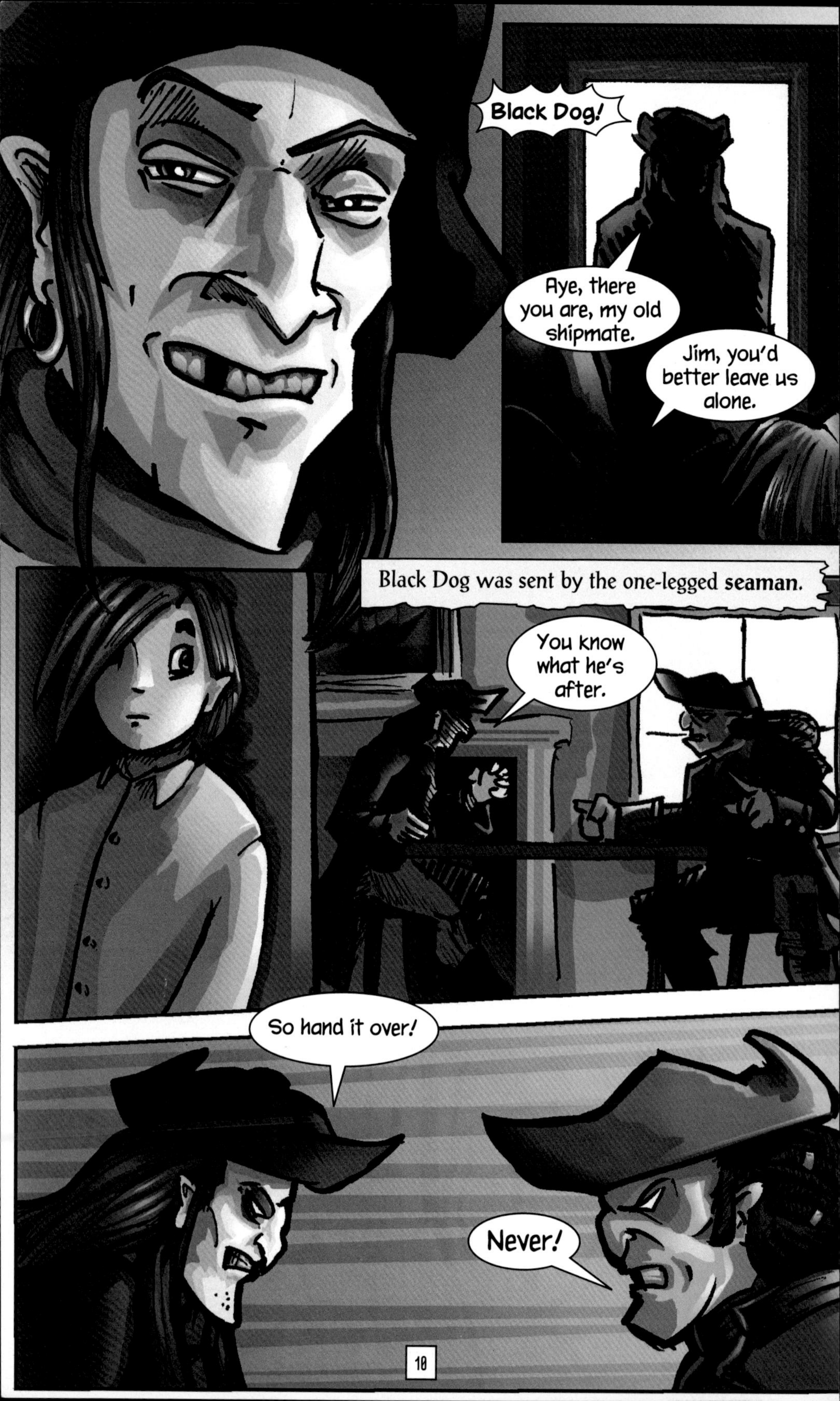
Black Dog!
Aye, there you are, my old shipmate.
Jim, you'd better leave us alone.
Black Dog was sent by the one-legged seaman.
You know what he's after.
So hand it over!
Never!

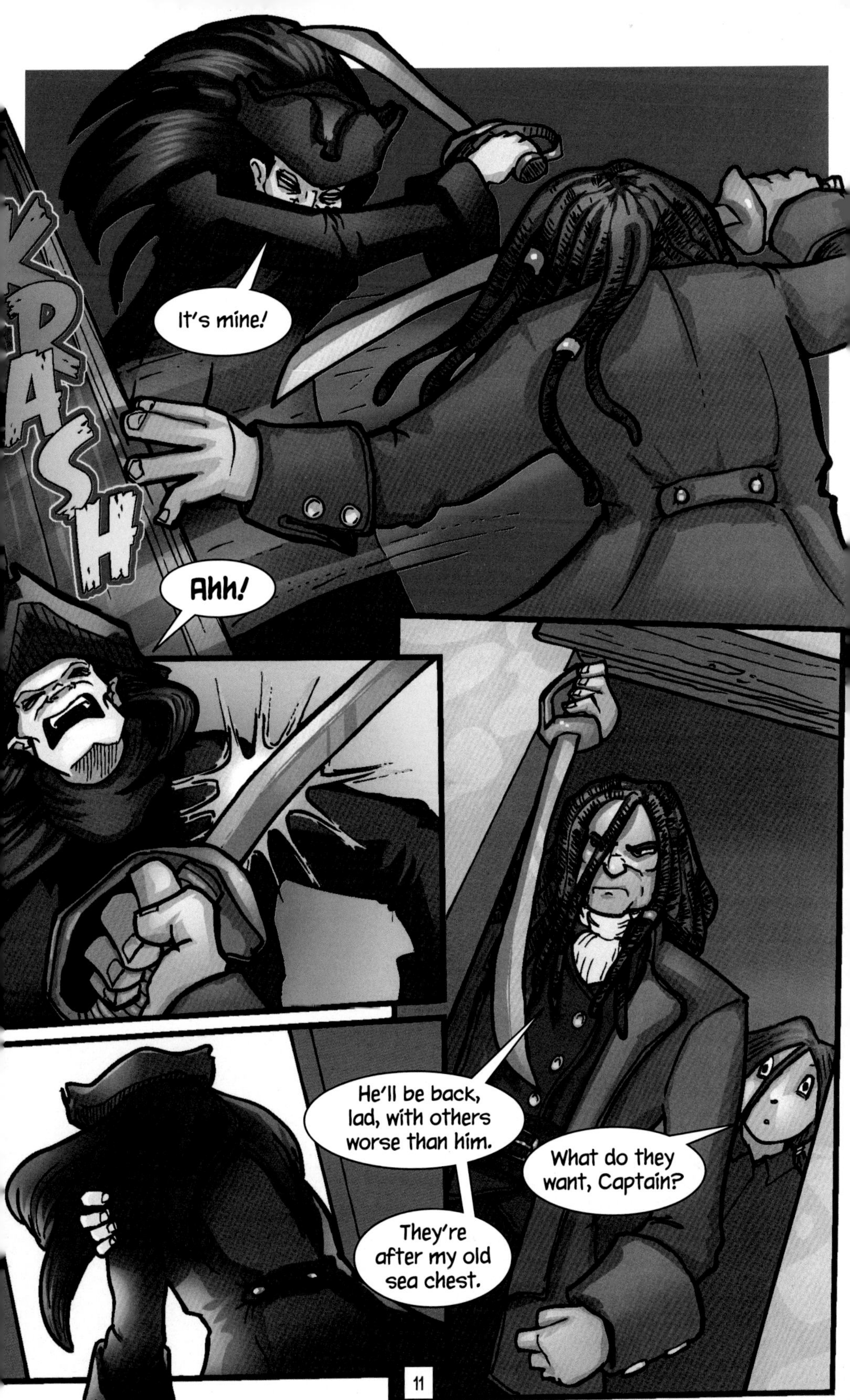
KRASH
It's mine!
Ahh!
He'll be back, lad, with others worse than him.
What do they want, Captain?
They're after my old sea chest.

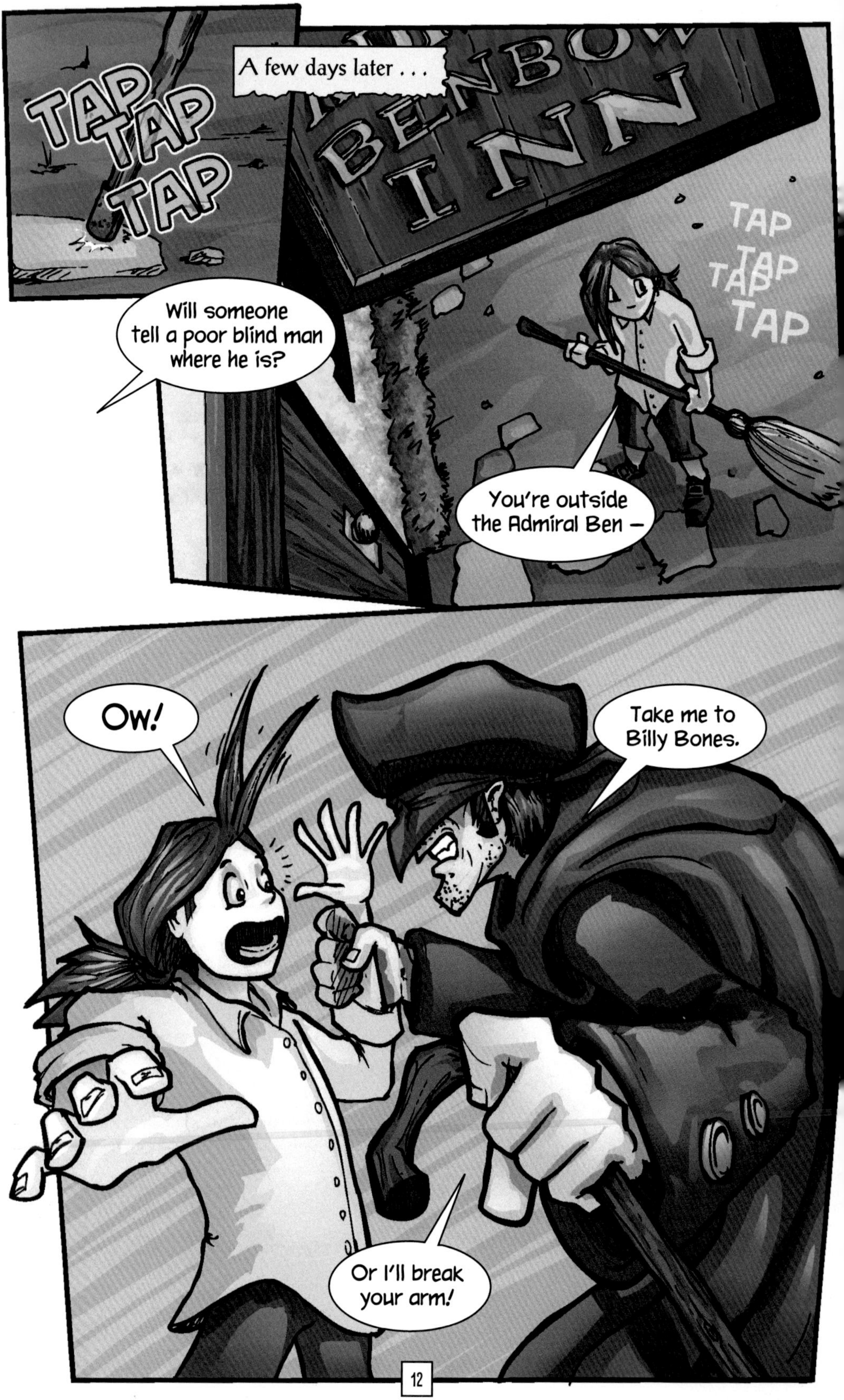
A few days later . . .
TAP TAP TAP
BENBOW
INN
Will someone tell a poor blind man where he is?
TAP TAP TAP TAP
You're outside the Admiral Ben –
Ow!
Take me to Billy Bones.
Or I'll break your arm!

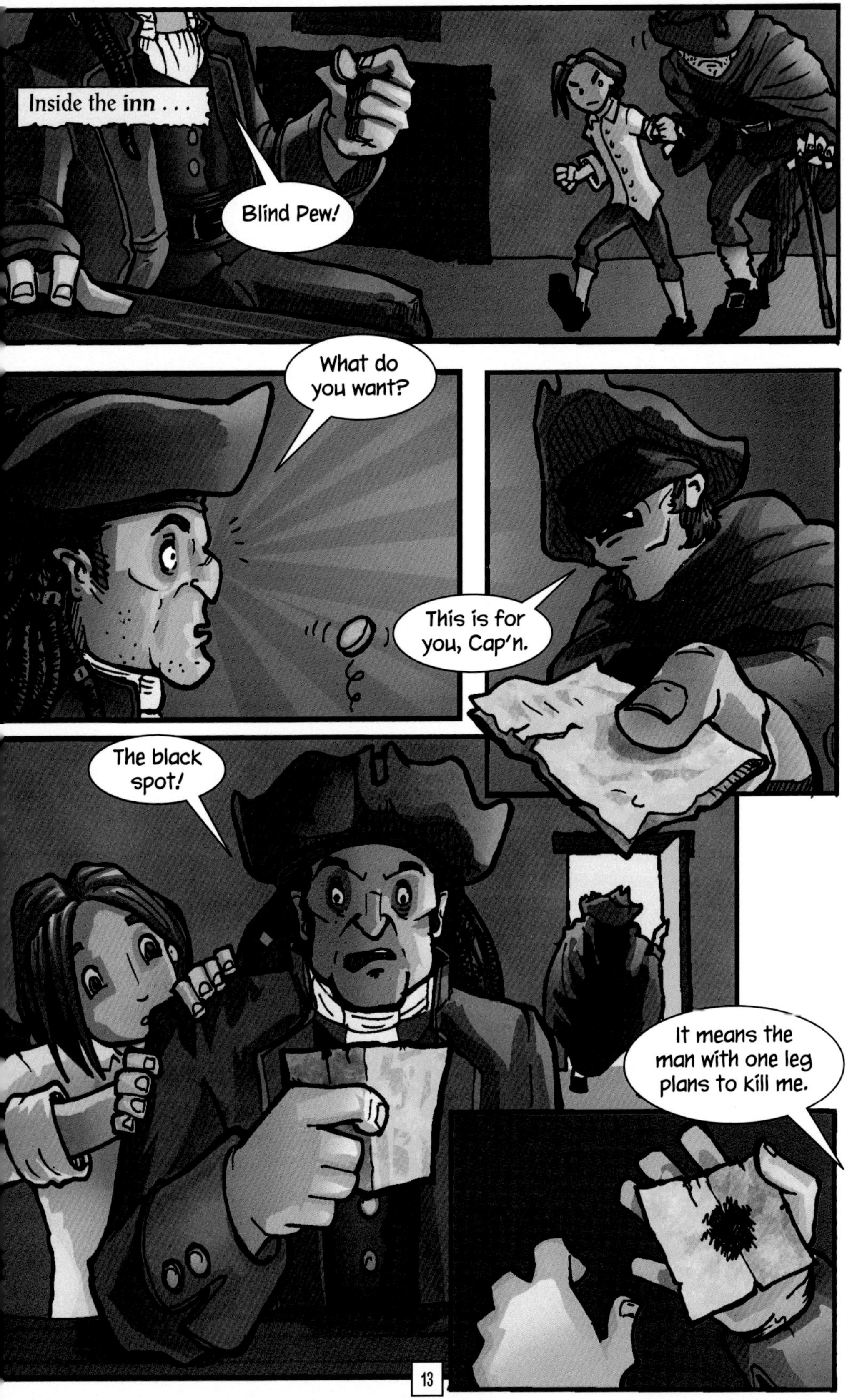
Inside the inn . . .
Blind Pew!
What do you want?
This is for you, Cap'n.
The black spot!
It means the man with one leg plans to kill me.

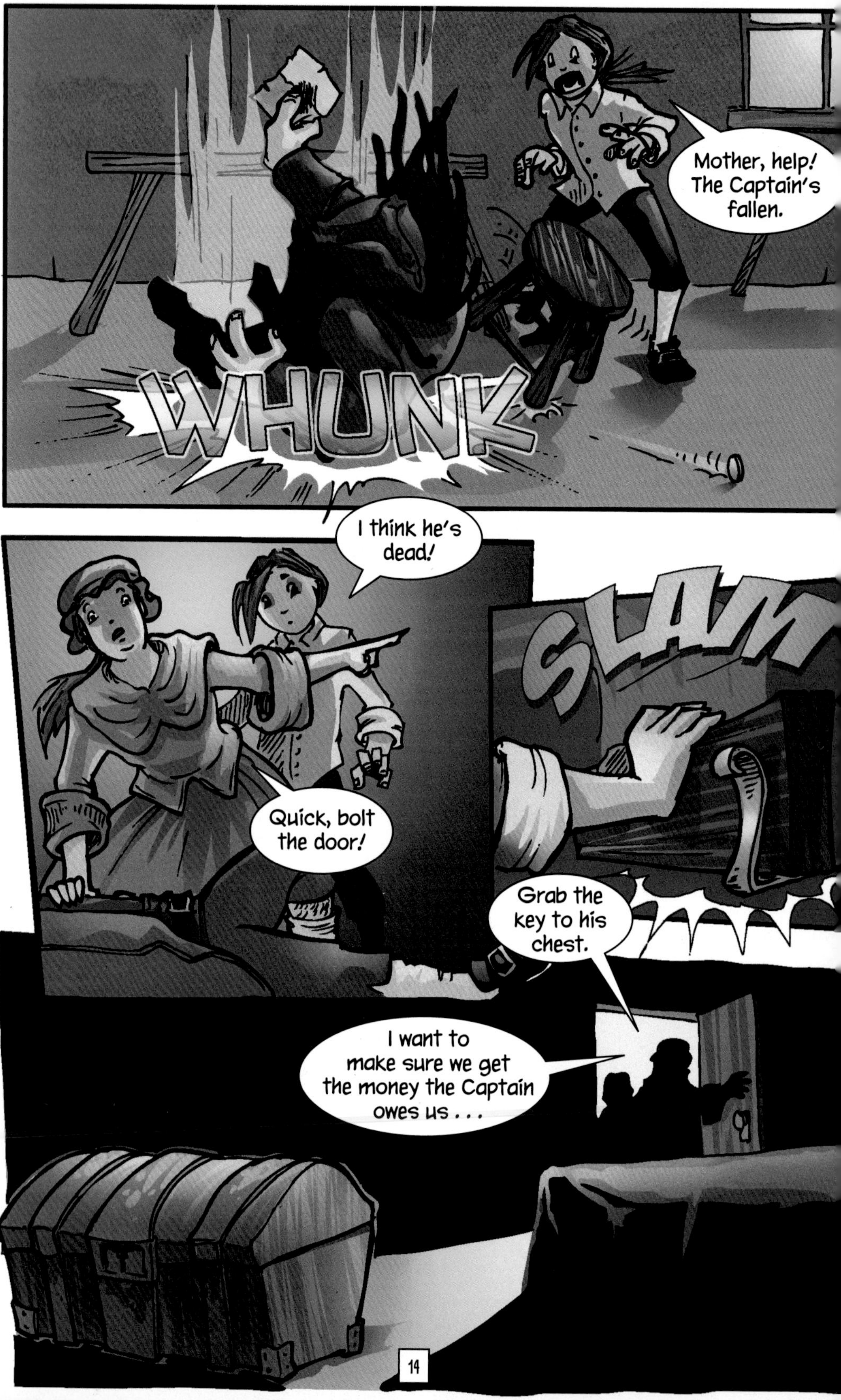
Mother, help! The Captain's fallen.
WHUNK
I think he's dead!
Quick, bolt the door!
Grab the key to his chest.
I want to make sure we get the money the Captain owes us . . .

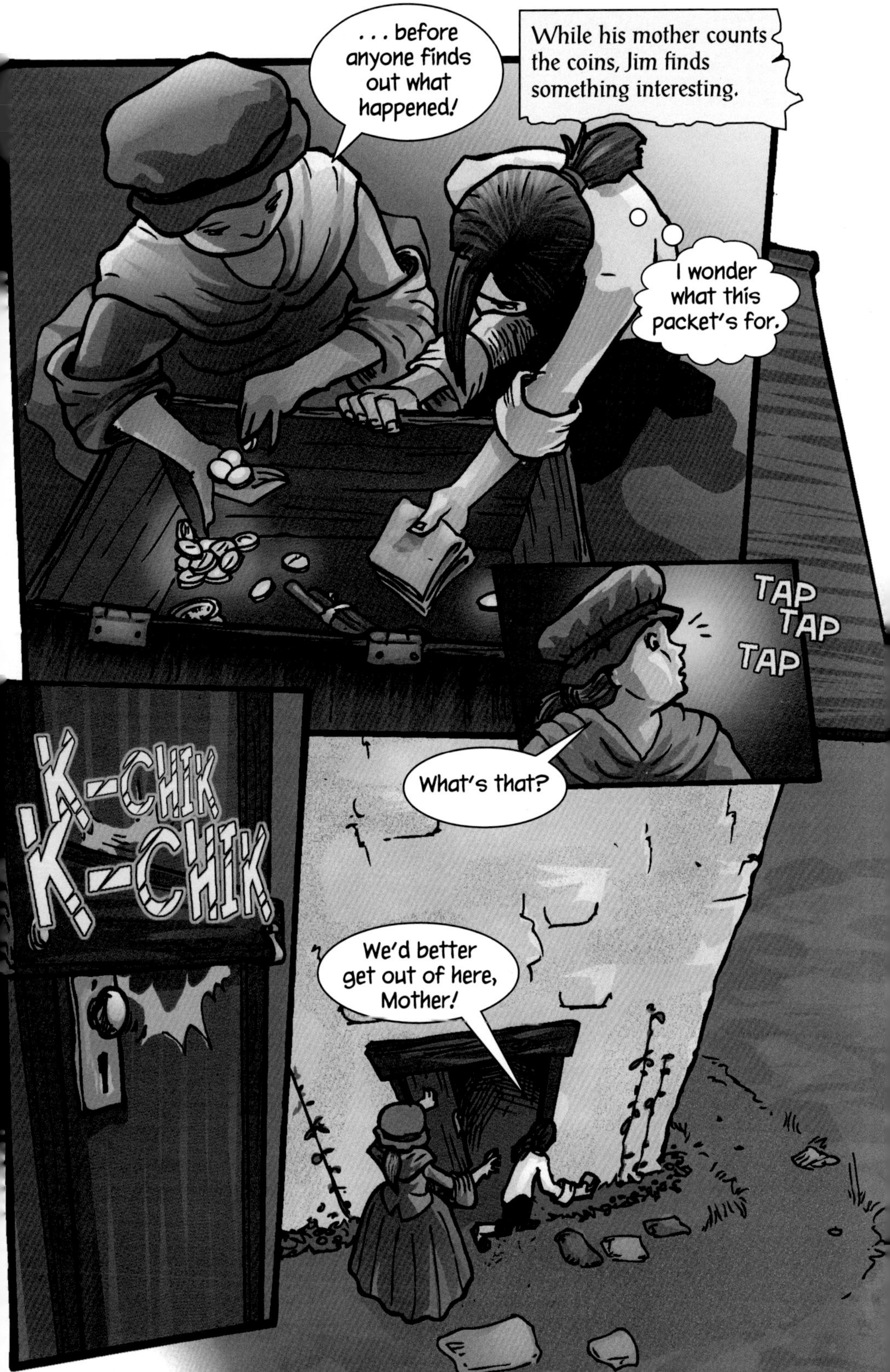

. . . before anyone finds out what happened!
While his mother counts the coins, Jim finds something interesting.
I wonder what this packet's for.
TAP TAP TAP
What's that?
K-CHIK K-CHIK
We'd better get out of here, Mother!

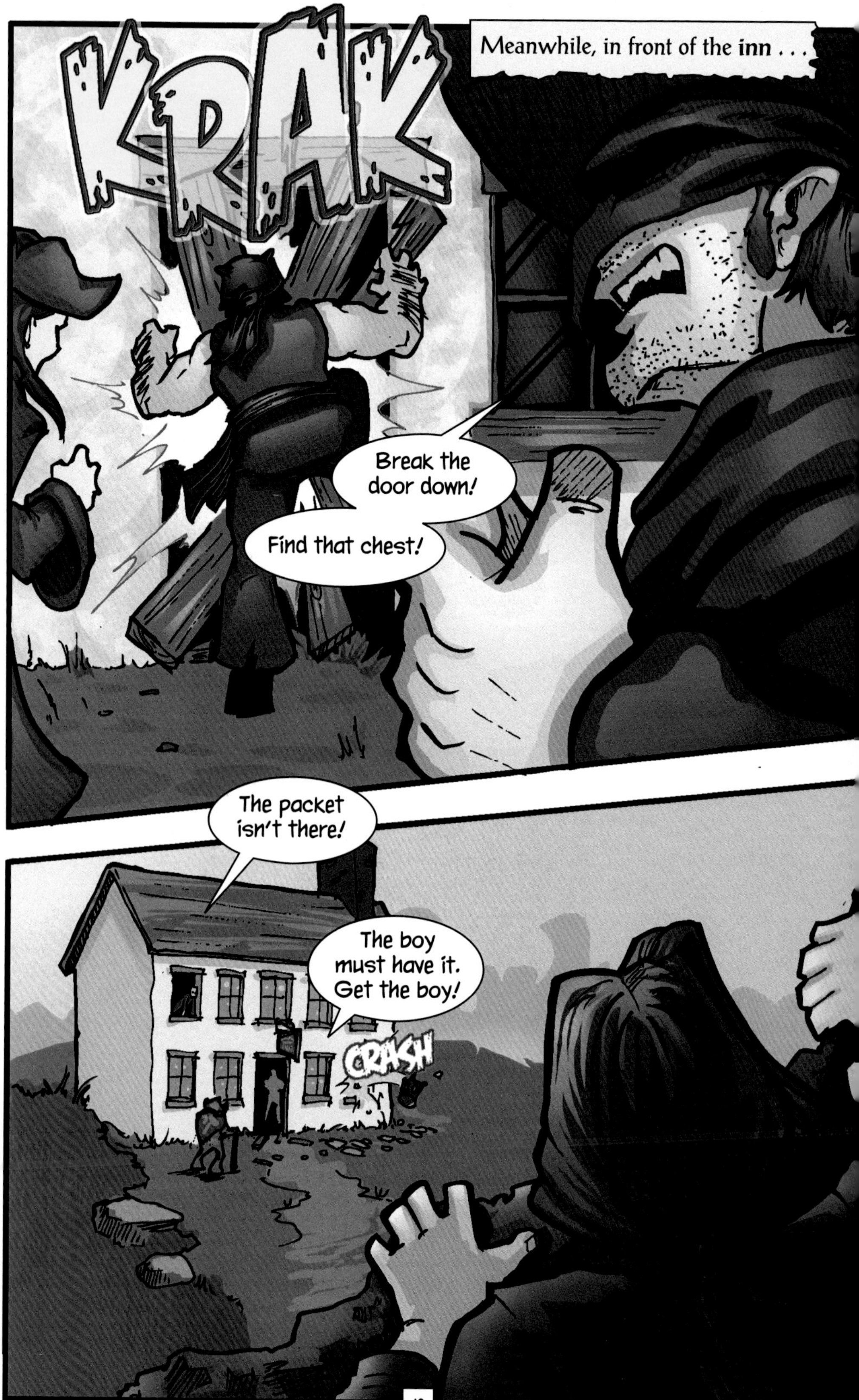
KRAK
Meanwhile, in front of the inn . . .
Break the door down!
Find that chest!
The packet isn't there!
The boy must have it. Get the boy!
CRASH

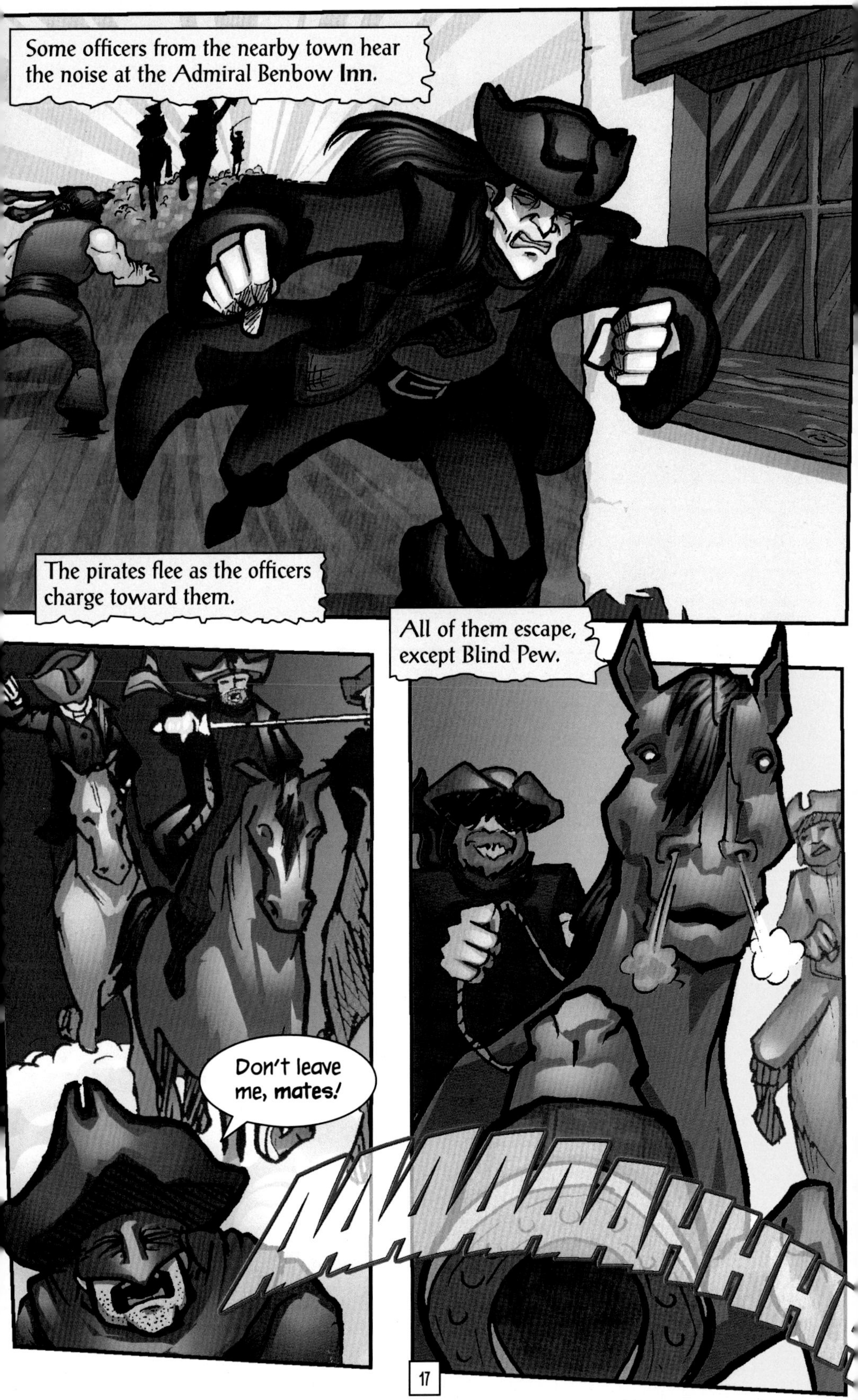

Some officers from the nearby town hear the noise at the Admiral Benbow Inn.
The pirates flee as the officers charge toward them.
All of them escape, except Blind Pew.
Don't leave me, mates!
AAAAAAHHH!

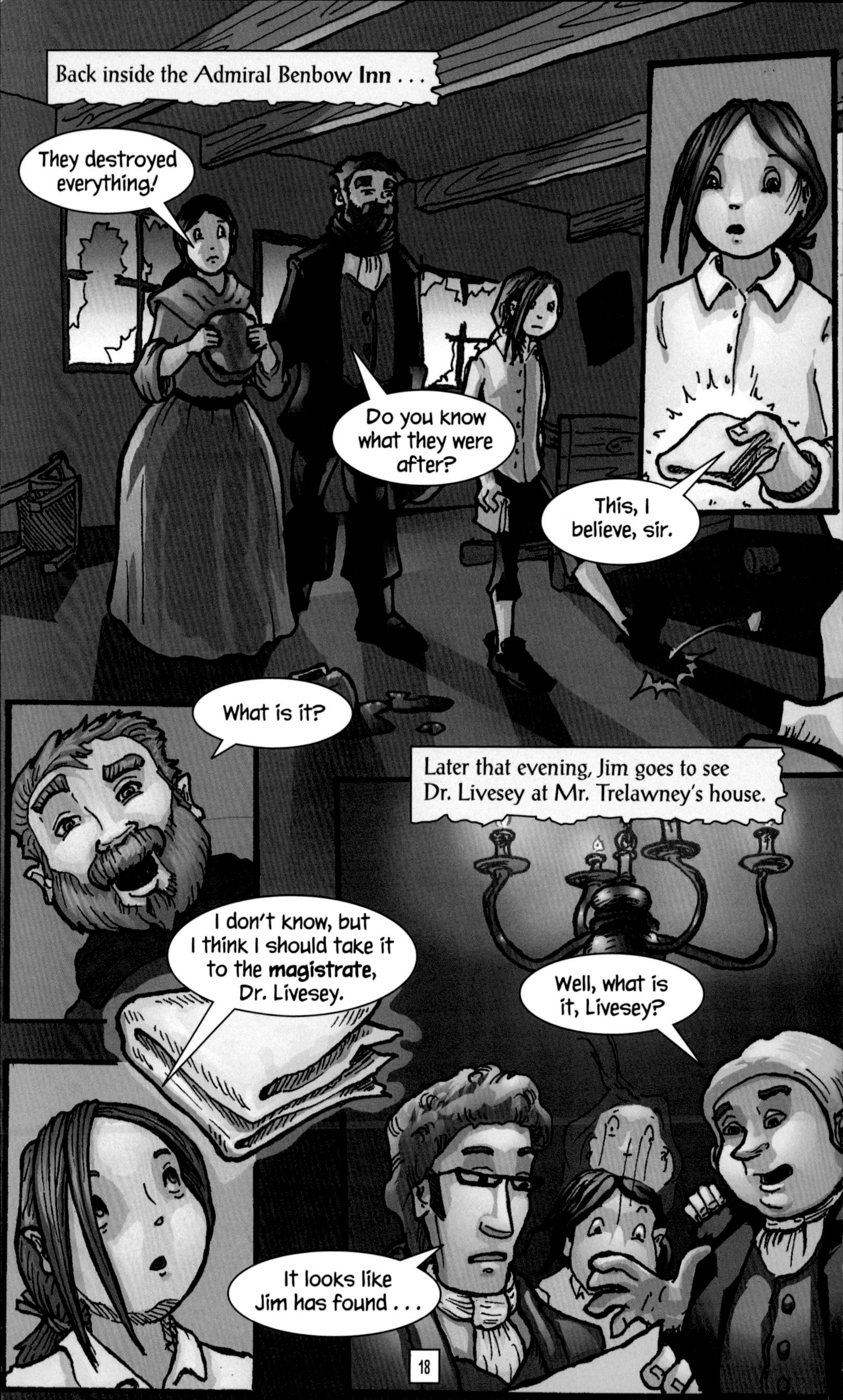
Back inside the Admiral Benbow Inn . . .
They destroyed everything!
Do you know what they were after?
This, I believe, sir.
What is it?
I don't know, but I think I should take it to the **magistrate**, Dr. Livesey.
Later that evening, Jim goes to see Dr. Livesey at Mr. Trelawney's house.
Well, what is it, Livesey?
It looks like Jim has found . . .

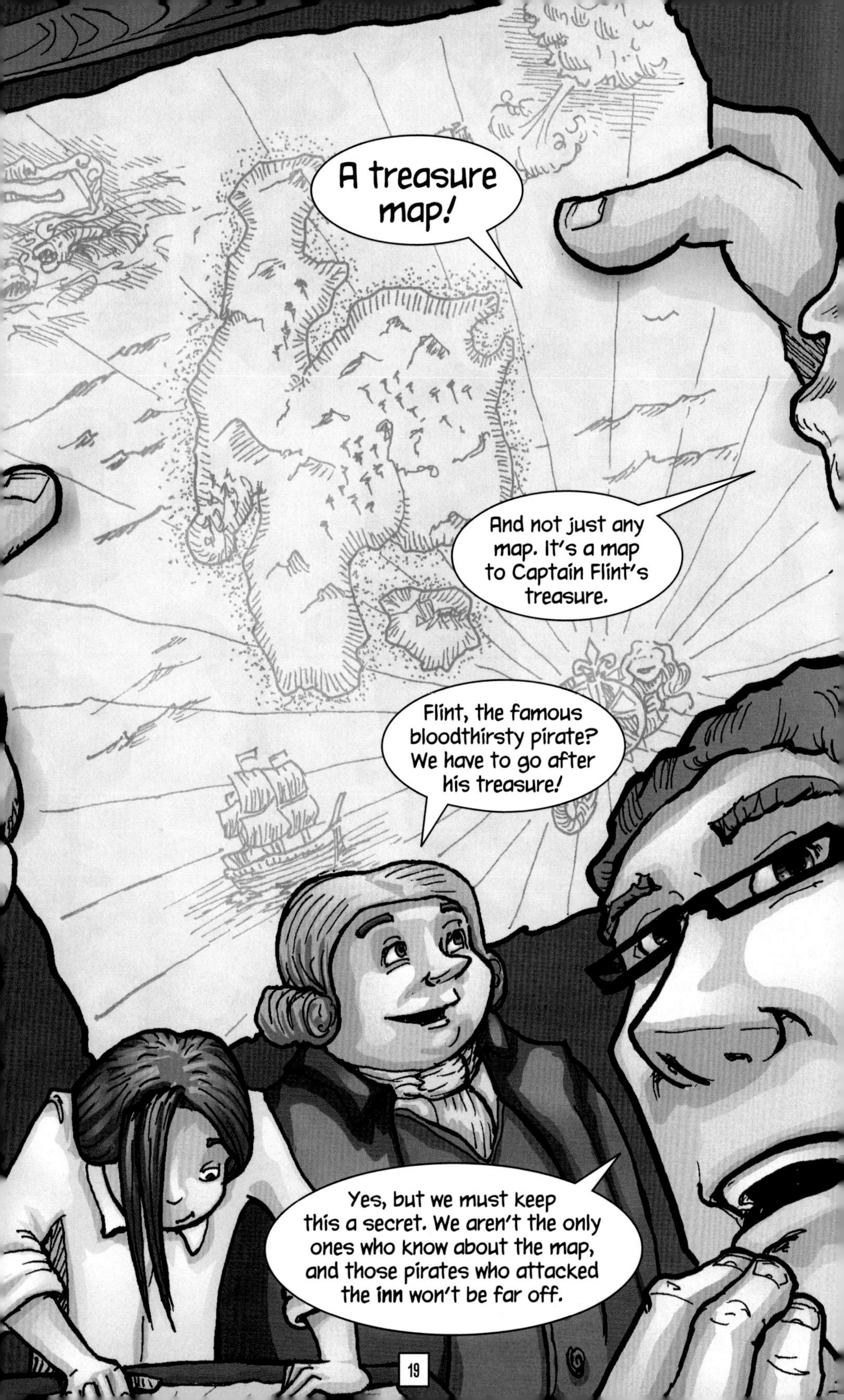
A treasure map!
And not just any map. It's a map to Captain Flint's treasure.
Flint, the famous bloodthirsty pirate? We have to go after his treasure!
Yes, but we must keep this a secret. We aren't the only ones who know about the map, and those pirates who attacked the inn won't be far off.

CHAPTER 2 The Sea Cook

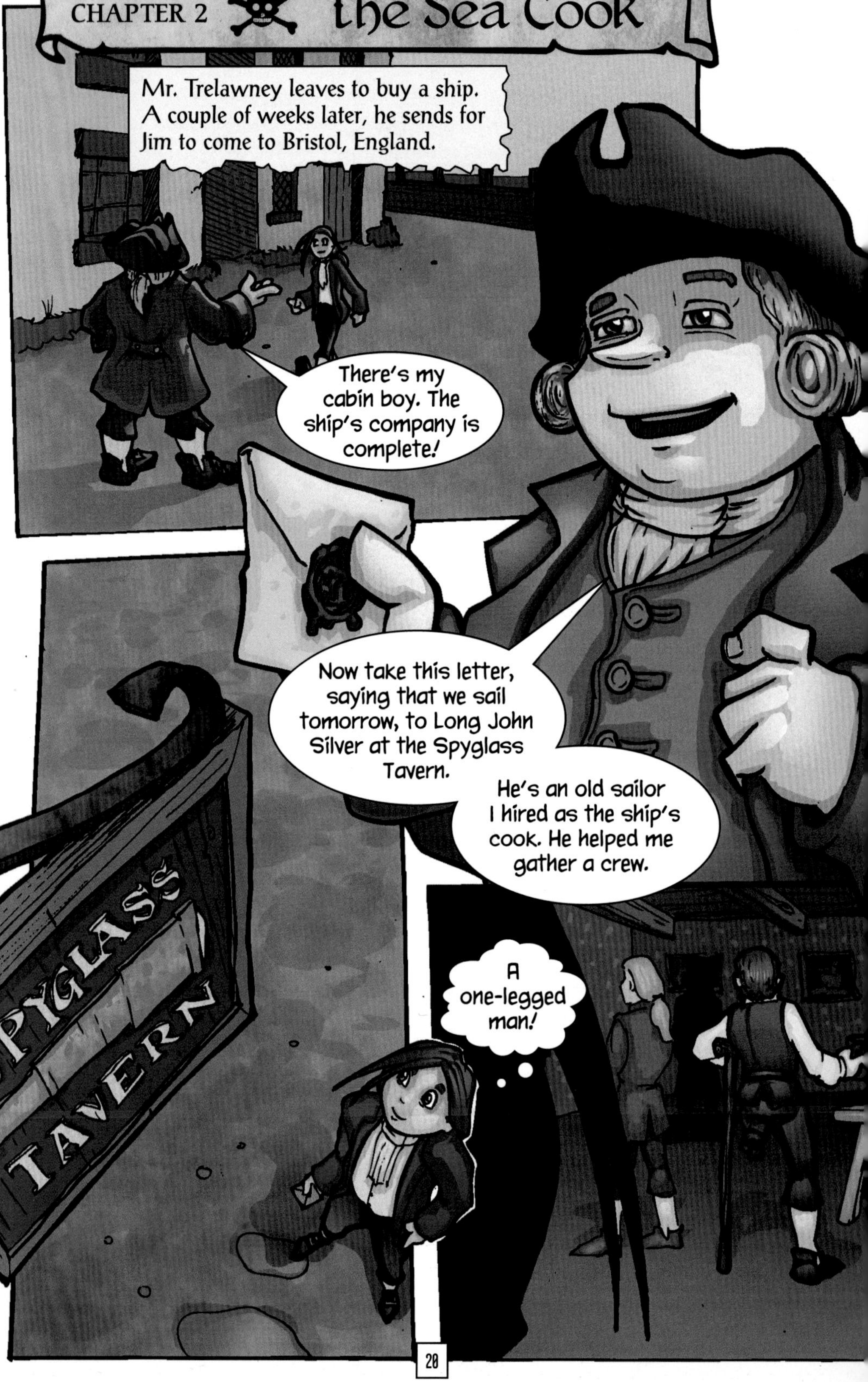
Mr. Trelawney leaves to buy a ship. A couple of weeks later, he sends for Jim to come to Bristol, England.
There's my cabin boy. The ship's company is complete!
Now take this letter, saying that we sail tomorrow, to Long John Silver at the Spyglass Tavern.
He's an old sailor I hired as the ship's cook. He helped me gather a crew.
PYGLASS
TAVERN
A one-legged man!

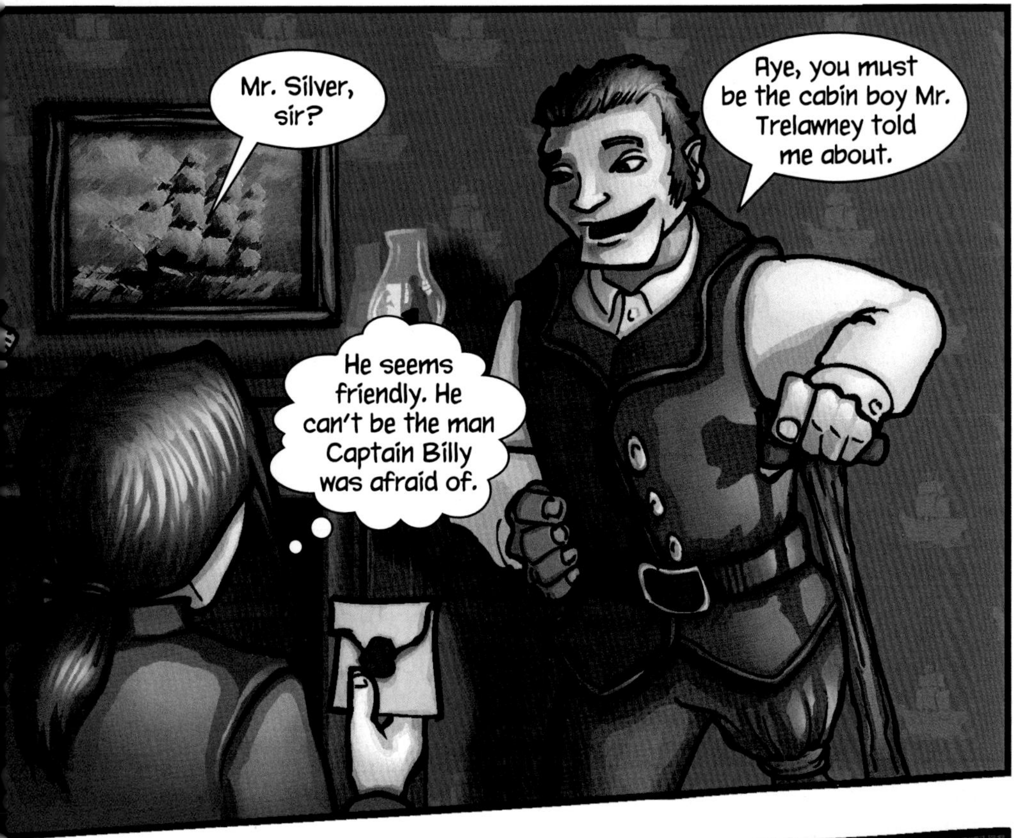
Mr. Silver, sir?
Aye, you must be the cabin boy Mr. Trelawney told me about.
He seems friendly. He can't be the man Captain Billy was afraid of.

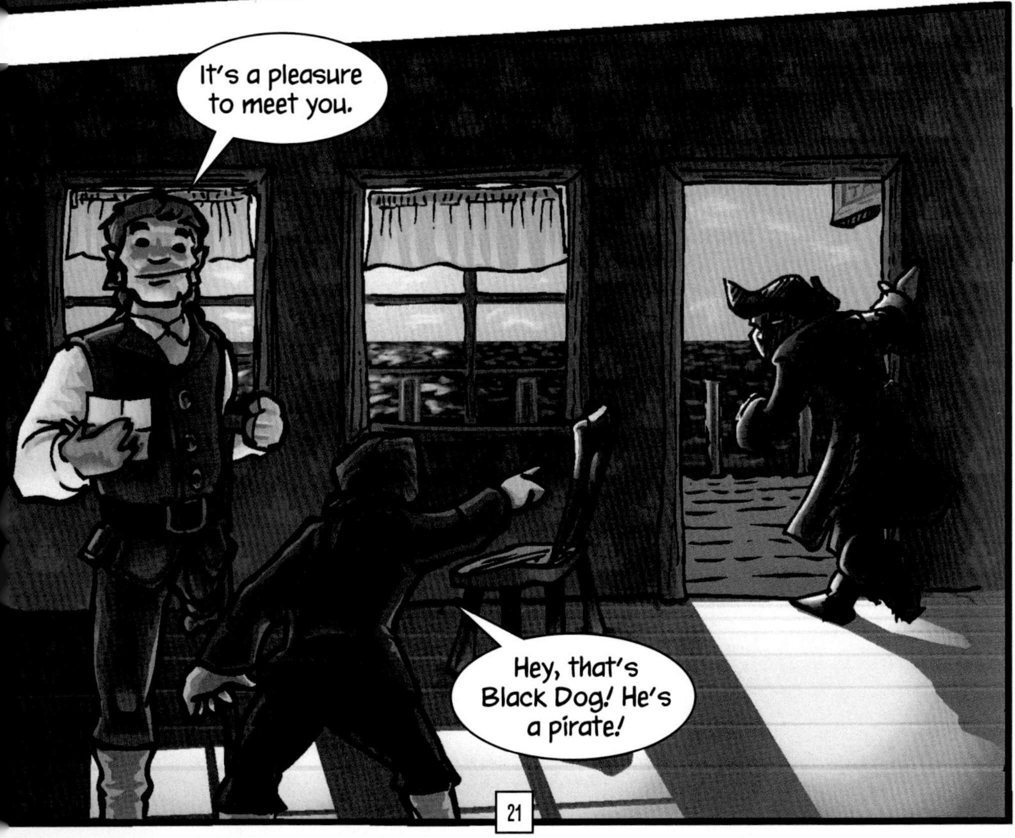
It's a pleasure to meet you.
Hey, that's Black Dog! He's a pirate!

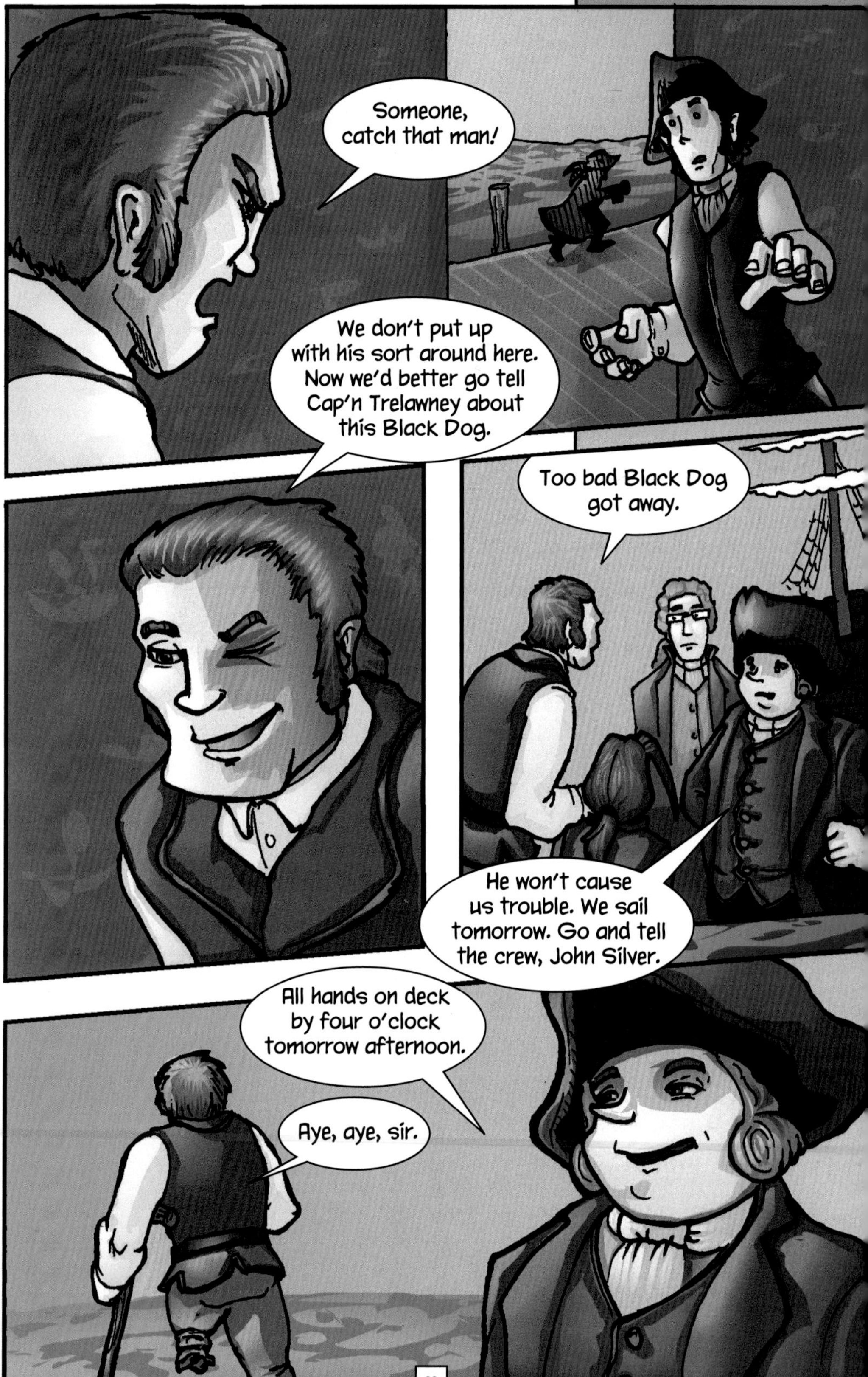
Someone, catch that man!
We don't put up with his sort around here. Now we'd better go tell Cap'n Trelawney about this Black Dog.
Too bad Black Dog got away.
He won't cause us trouble. We sail tomorrow. Go and tell the crew, John Silver.
All hands on deck by four o'clock tomorrow afternoon.
Aye, aye, sir.

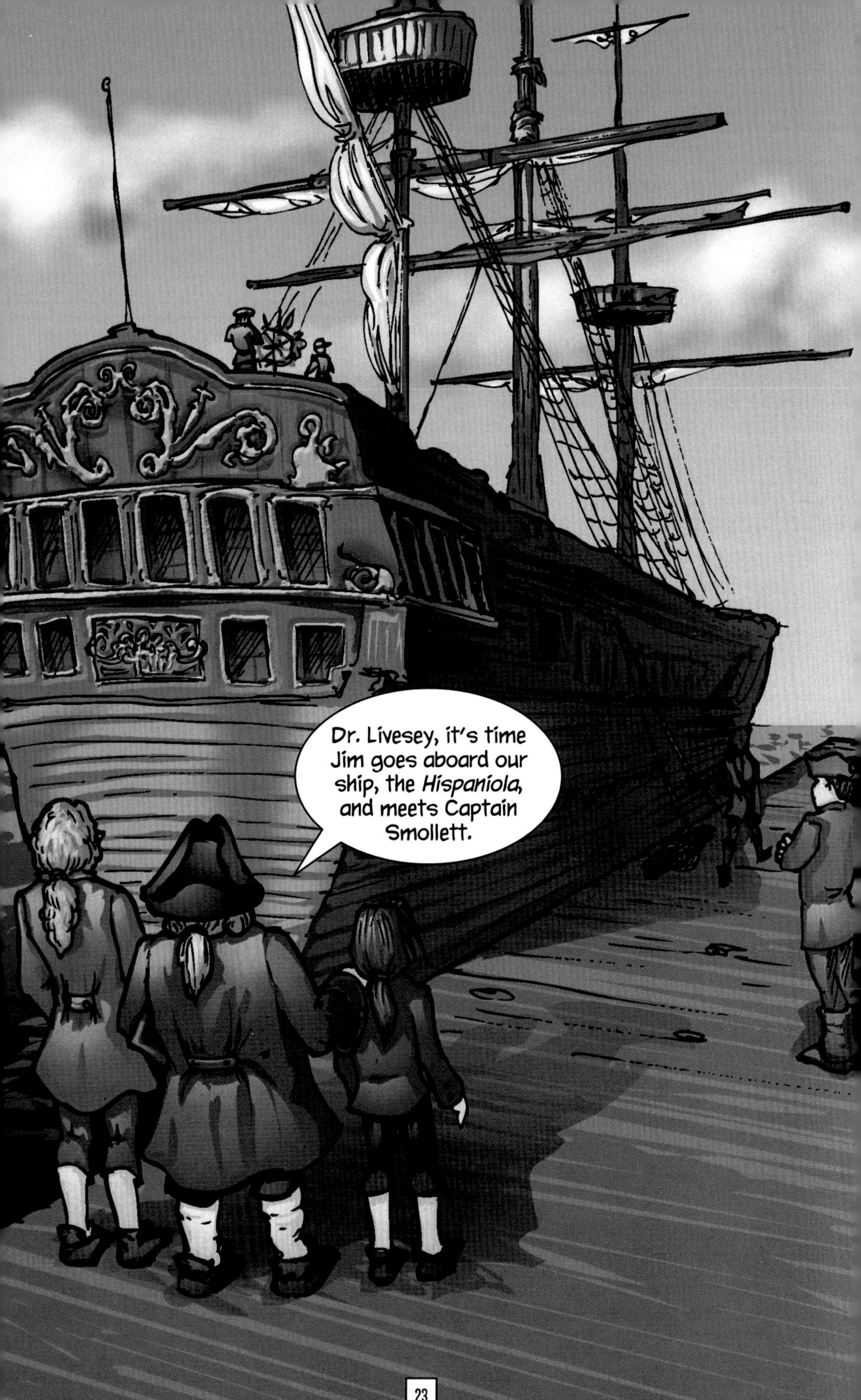
Dr. Livesey, it's time Jim goes aboard our ship, the *Hispaniola*, and meets Captain Smollett.

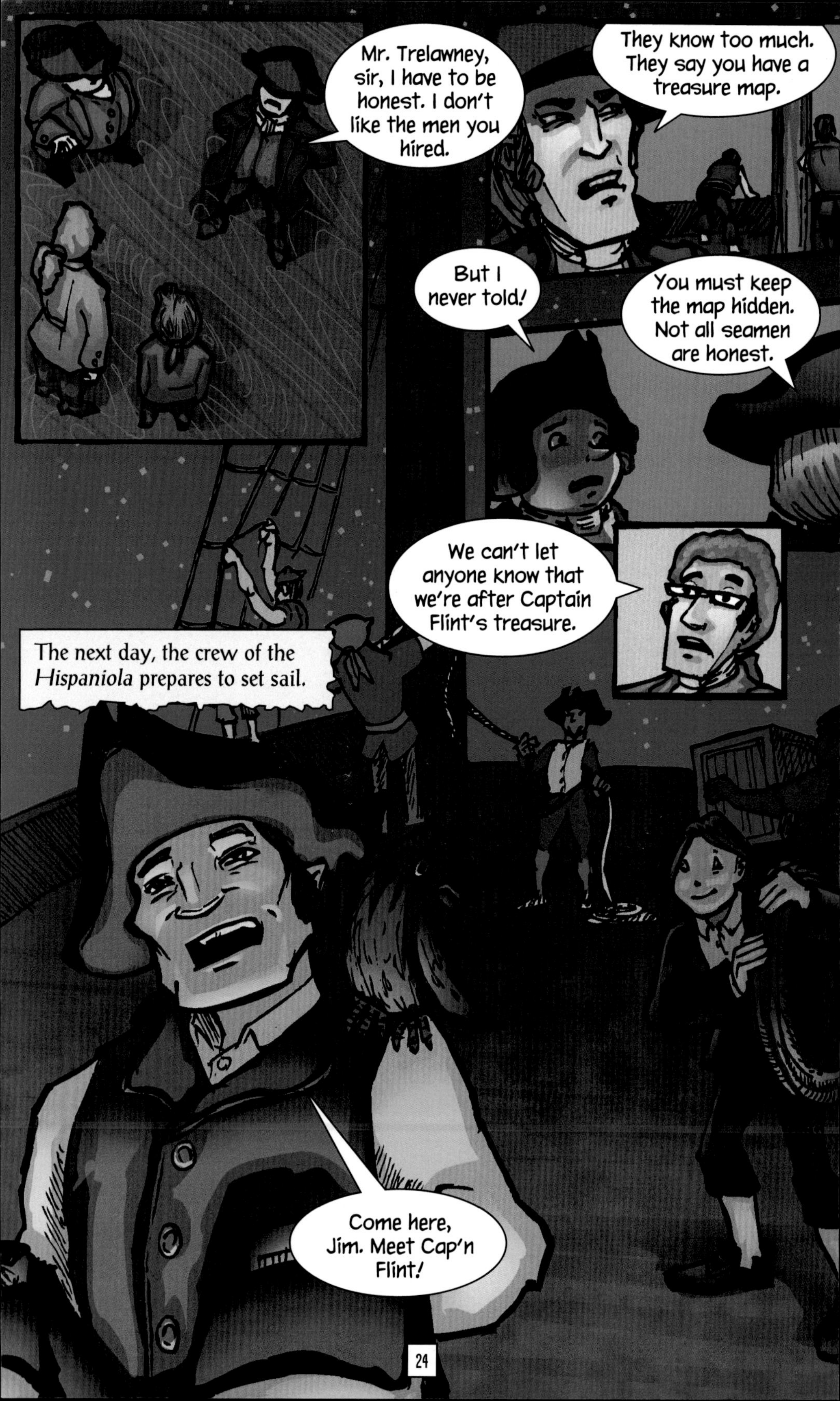
Mr. Trelawney, sir, I have to be honest. I don't like the men you hired.
They know too much. They say you have a treasure map.
But I never told!
You must keep the map hidden. Not all seamen are honest.
We can't let anyone know that we're after Captain Flint's treasure.
The next day, the crew of the *Hispaniola* prepares to set sail.
Come here, Jim. Meet Cap'n Flint!

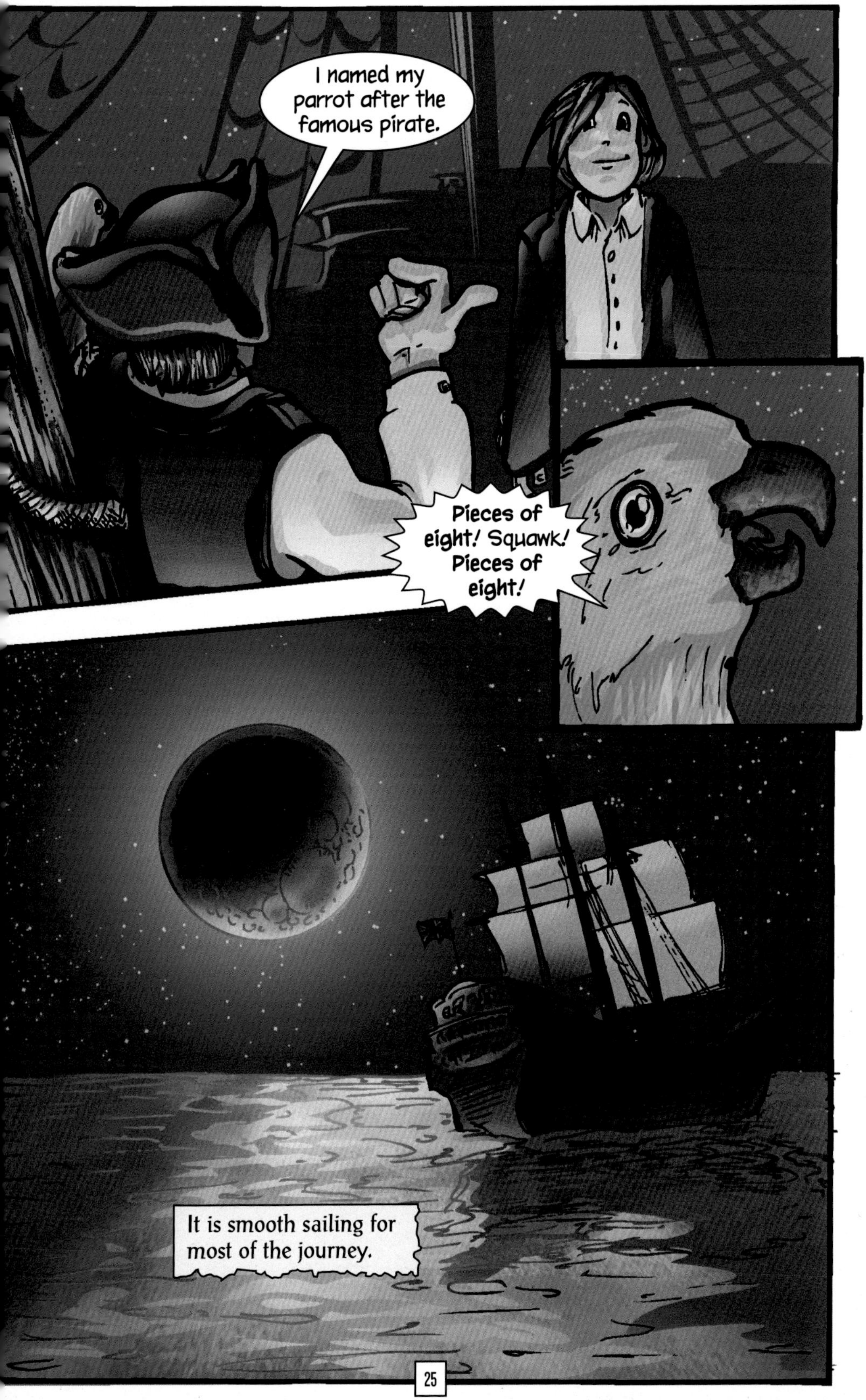
I named my parrot after the famous pirate.
Pieces of eight! Squawk! Pieces of eight!
It is smooth sailing for most of the journey.

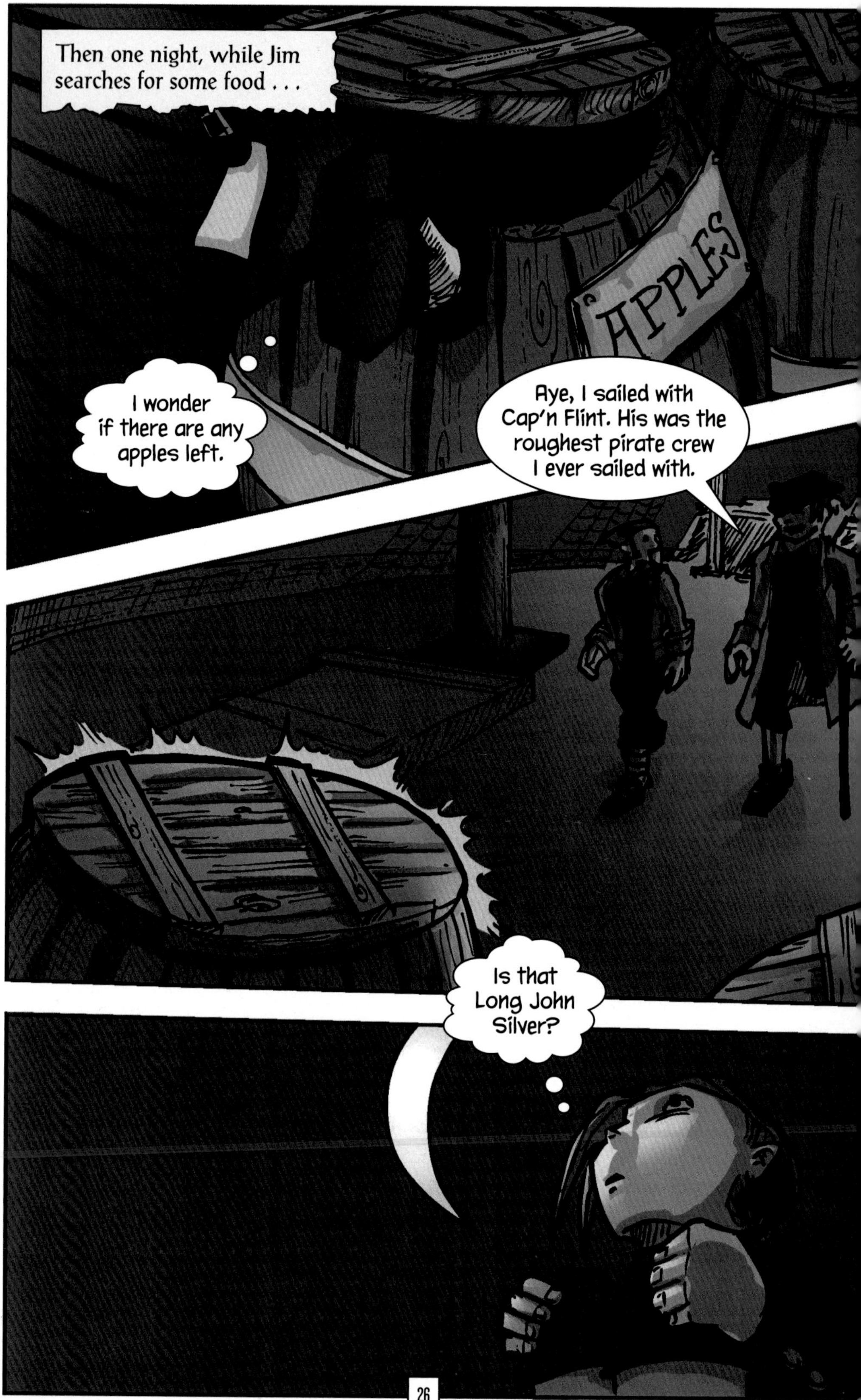

Then one night, while Jim searches for some food . . .
I wonder if there are any apples left.
APPLES
Aye, I sailed with Cap'n Flint. His was the roughest pirate crew I ever sailed with.
Is that Long John Silver?

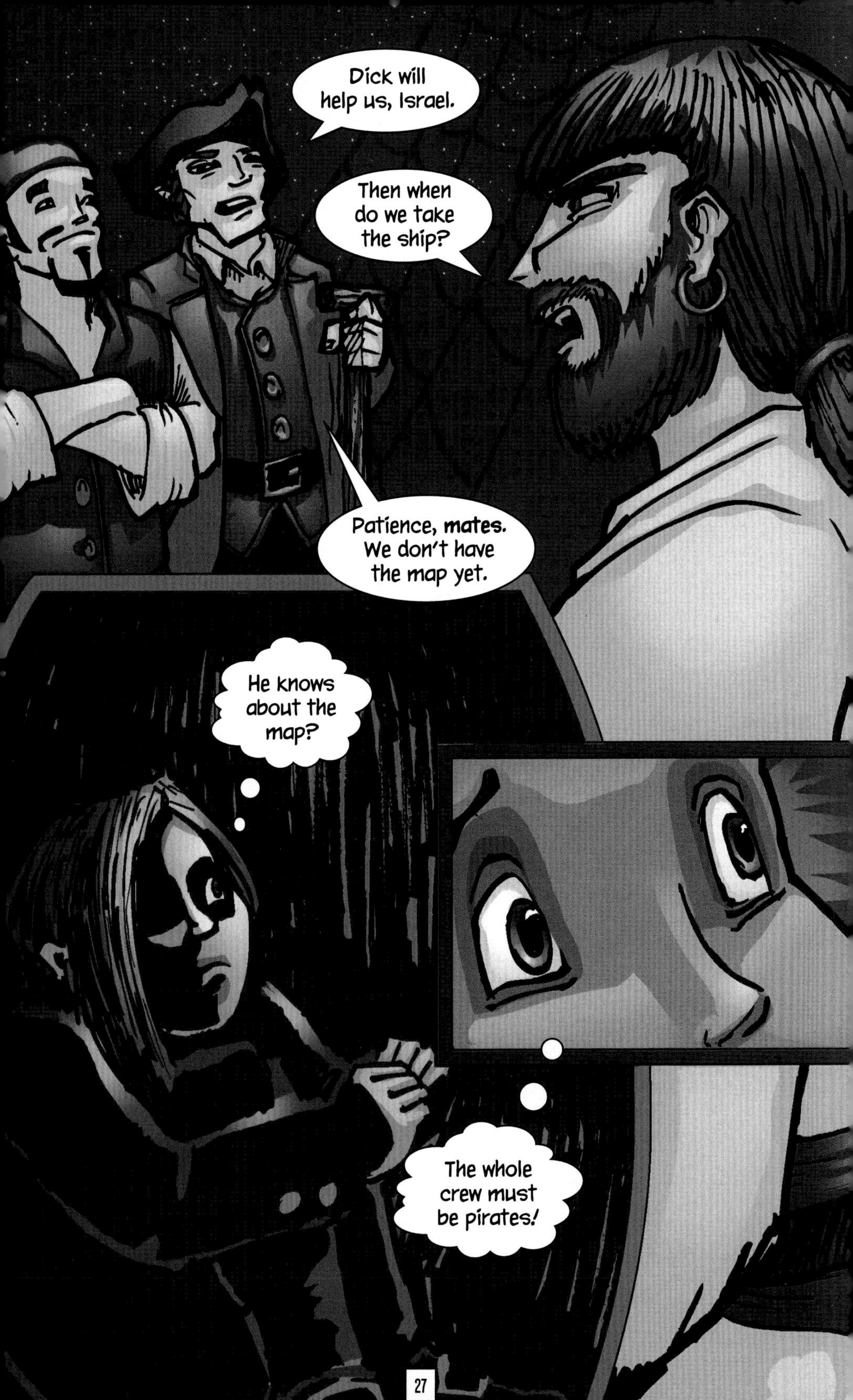
Dick will help us, Israel.
Then when do we take the ship?
Patience, mates. We don't have the map yet.
He knows about the map?
The whole crew must be pirates!

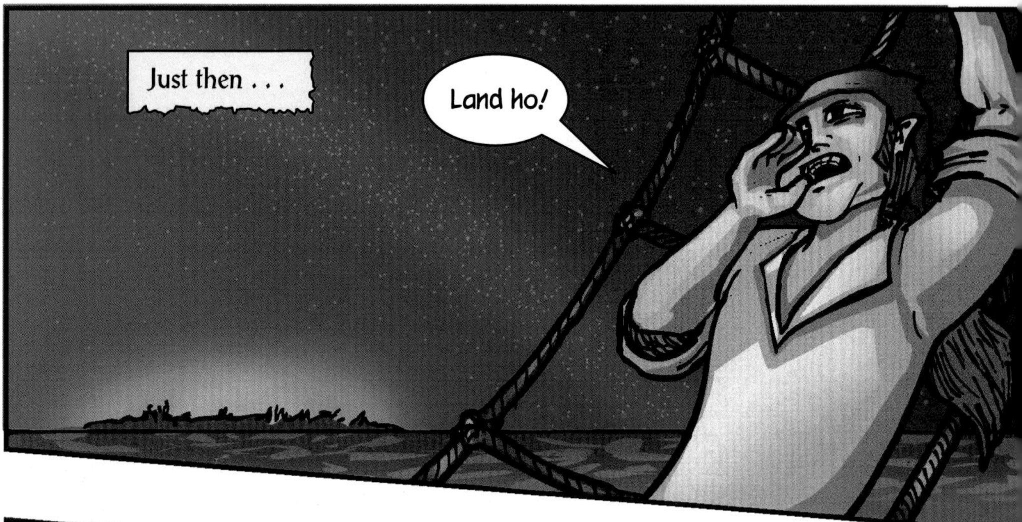
Just then . . .
Land ho!

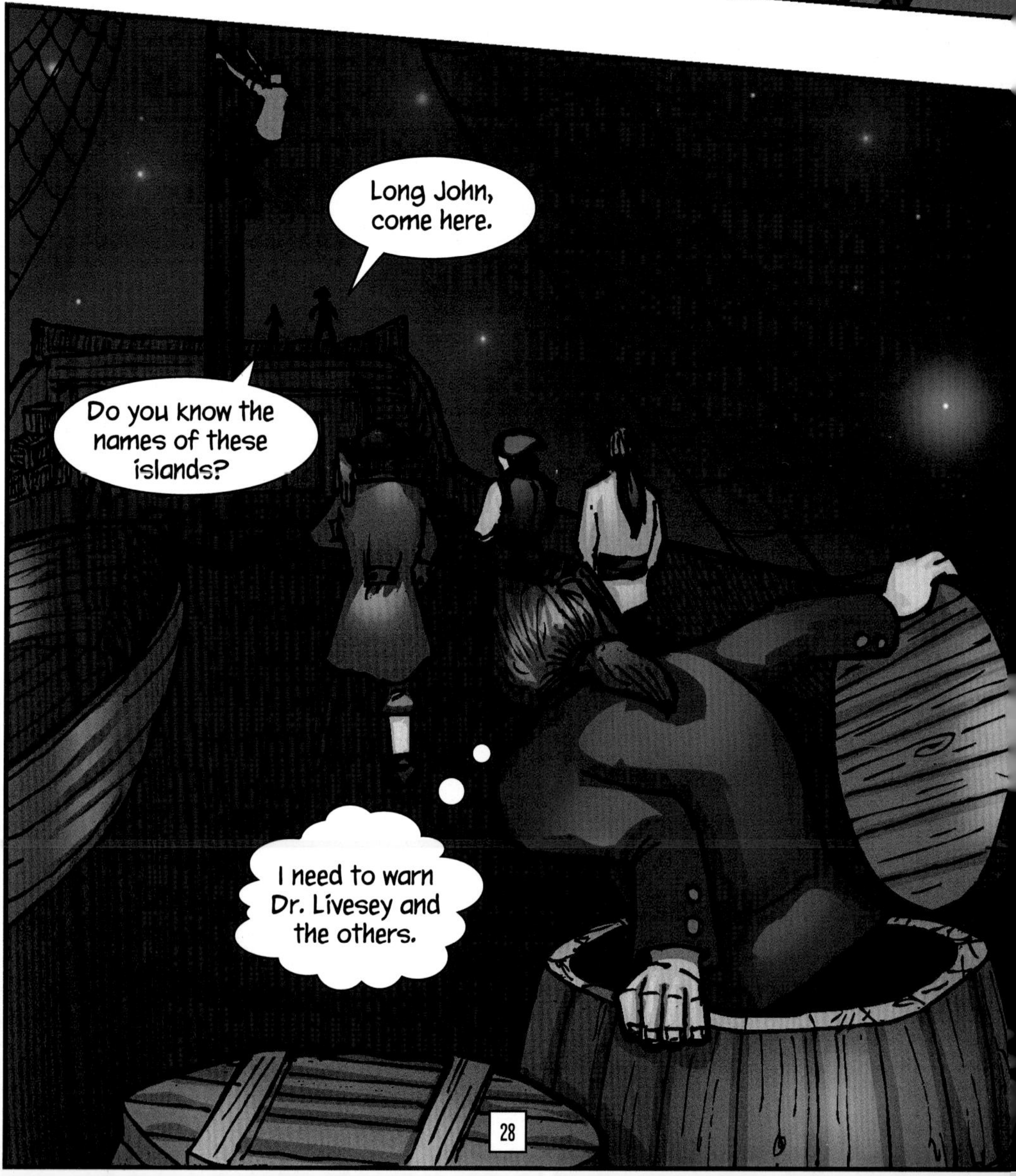
Long John, come here.
Do you know the names of these islands?
I need to warn Dr. Livesey and the others.

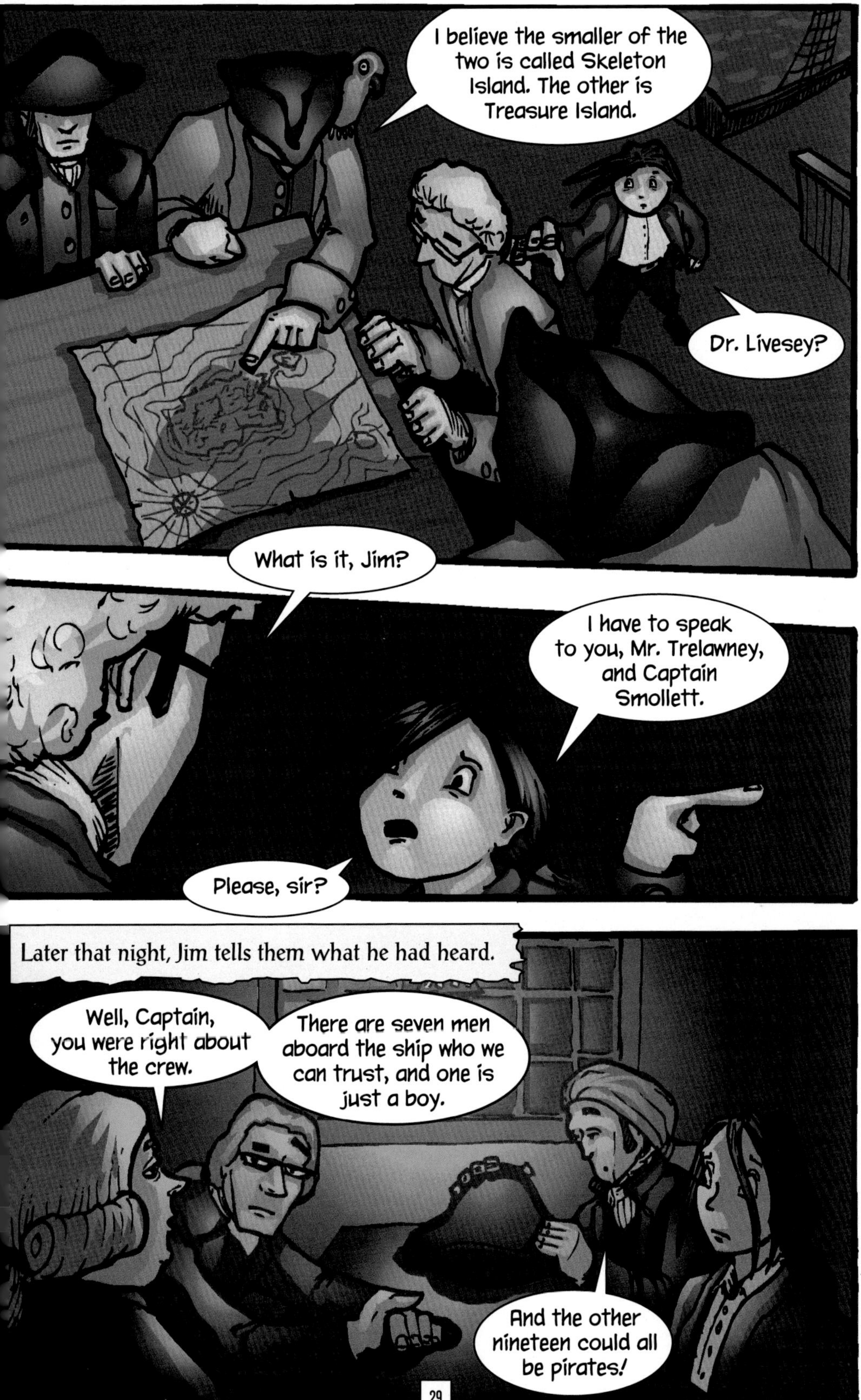
I believe the smaller of the two is called Skeleton Island. The other is Treasure Island.
Dr. Livesey?
What is it, Jim?
I have to speak to you, Mr. Trelawney, and Captain Smollett.
Please, sir?
Later that night, Jim tells them what he had heard.
Well, Captain, you were right about the crew.
There are seven men aboard the ship who we can trust, and one is just a boy.
And the other nineteen could all be pirates!

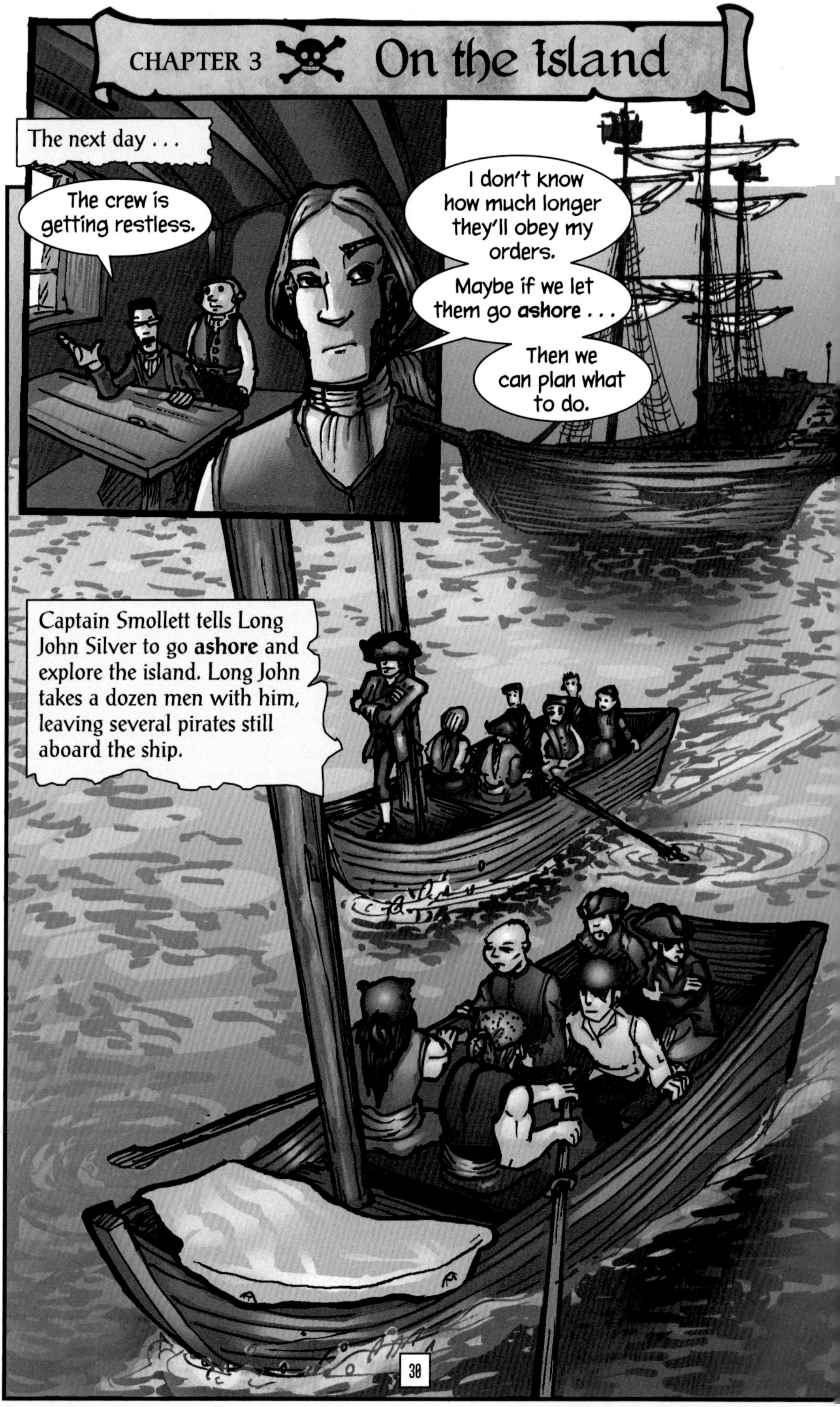
CHAPTER 3 On the Island
The next day . . .
The crew is getting restless.
I don't know how much longer they'll obey my orders.
Maybe if we let them go **ashore** . . .
Then we can plan what to do.
Captain Smollett tells Long John Silver to go **ashore** and explore the island. Long John takes a dozen men with him, leaving several pirates still aboard the ship.

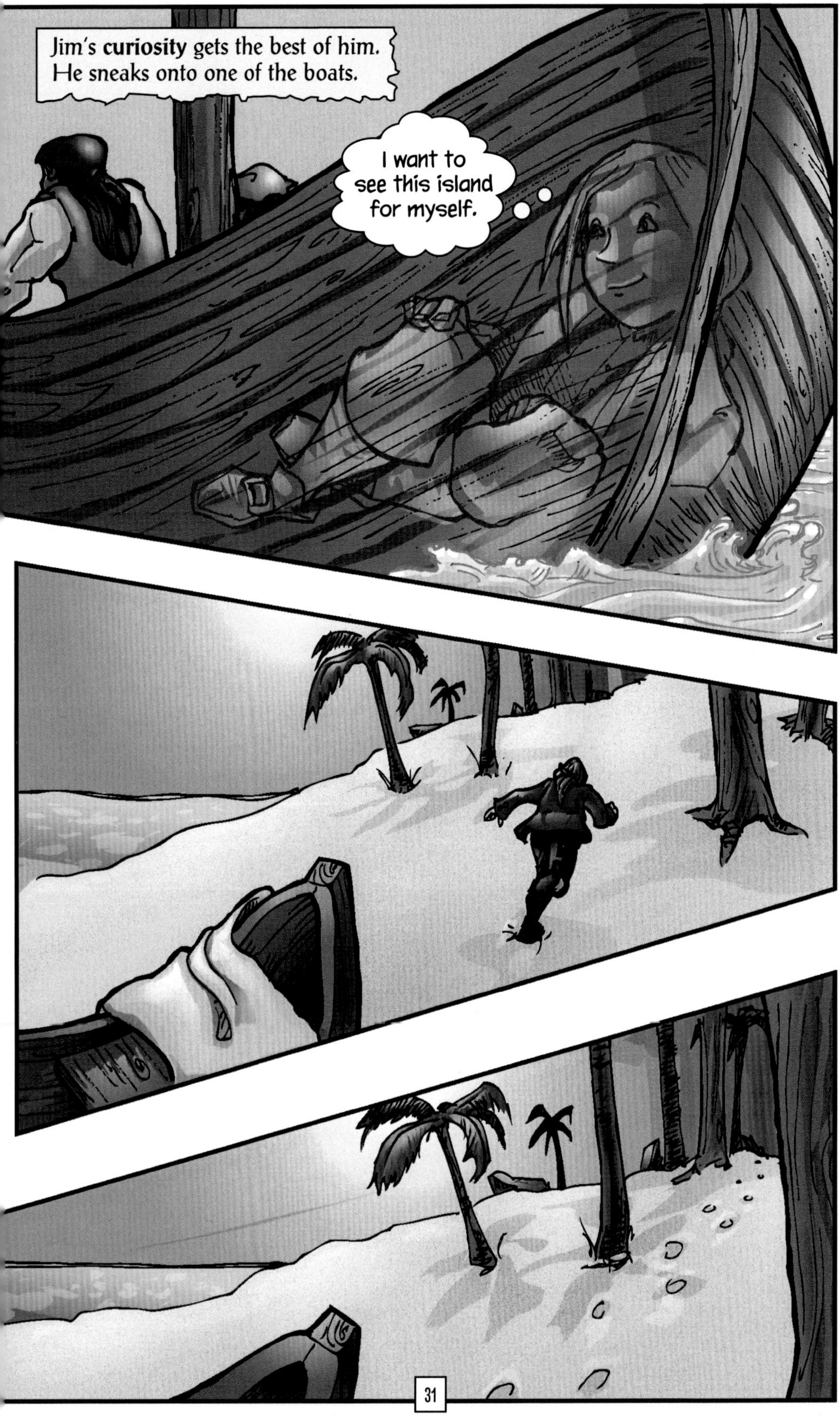

Jim's **curiosity** gets the best of him. He sneaks onto one of the boats.
I want to see this island for myself.

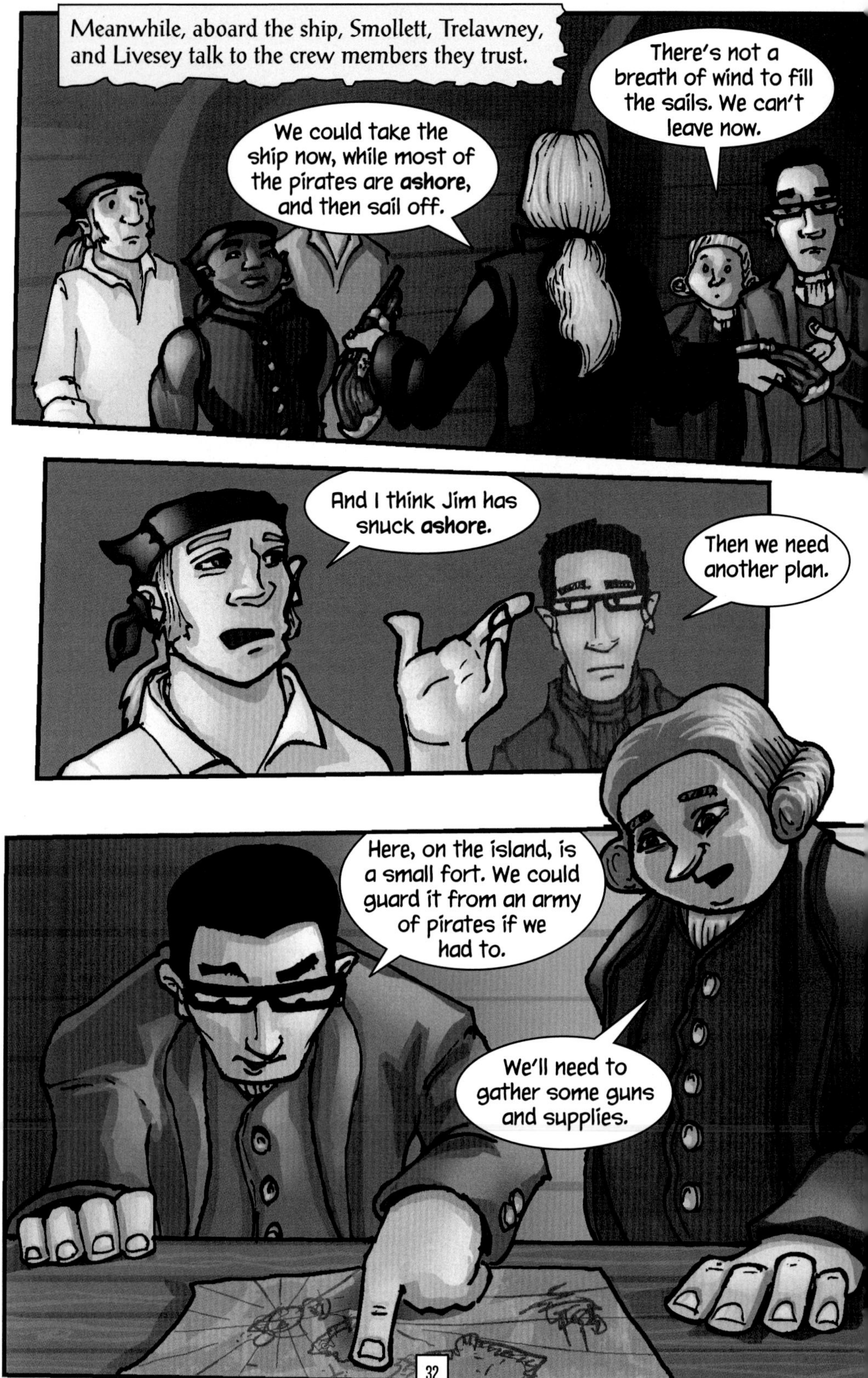
Meanwhile, aboard the ship, Smollett, Trelawney, and Livesey talk to the crew members they trust.
We could take the ship now, while most of the pirates are **ashore**, and then sail off.
There's not a breath of wind to fill the sails. We can't leave now.
And I think Jim has snuck **ashore**.
Then we need another plan.
Here, on the island, is a small fort. We could guard it from an army of pirates if we had to.
We'll need to gather some guns and supplies.

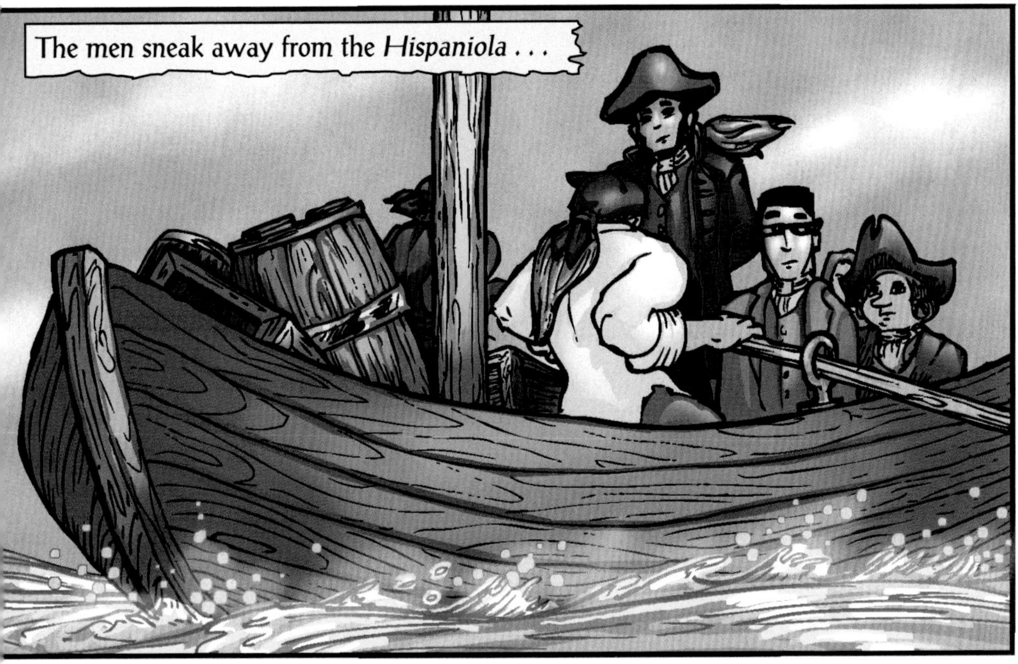
The men sneak away from the *Hispaniola* . . .

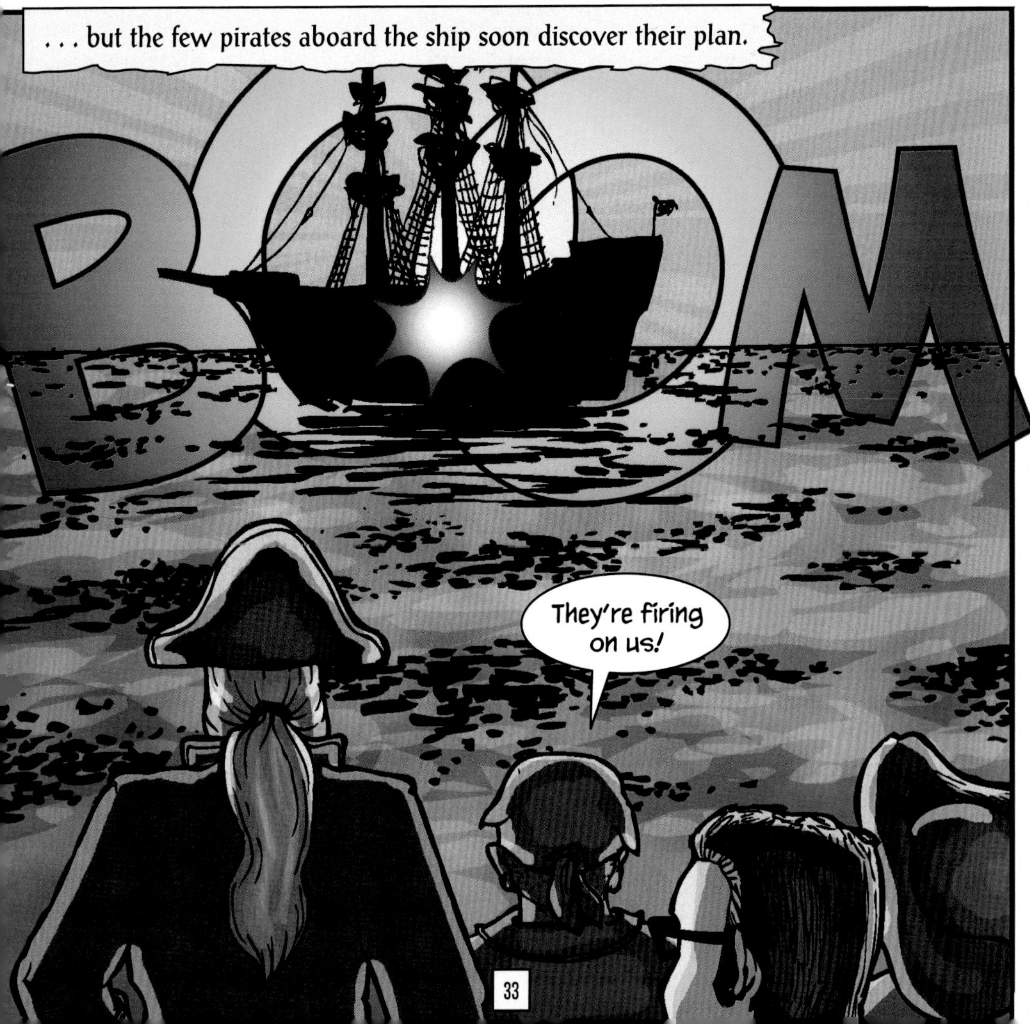
. . . but the few pirates aboard the ship soon discover their plan.
BOOM
They're firing on us!

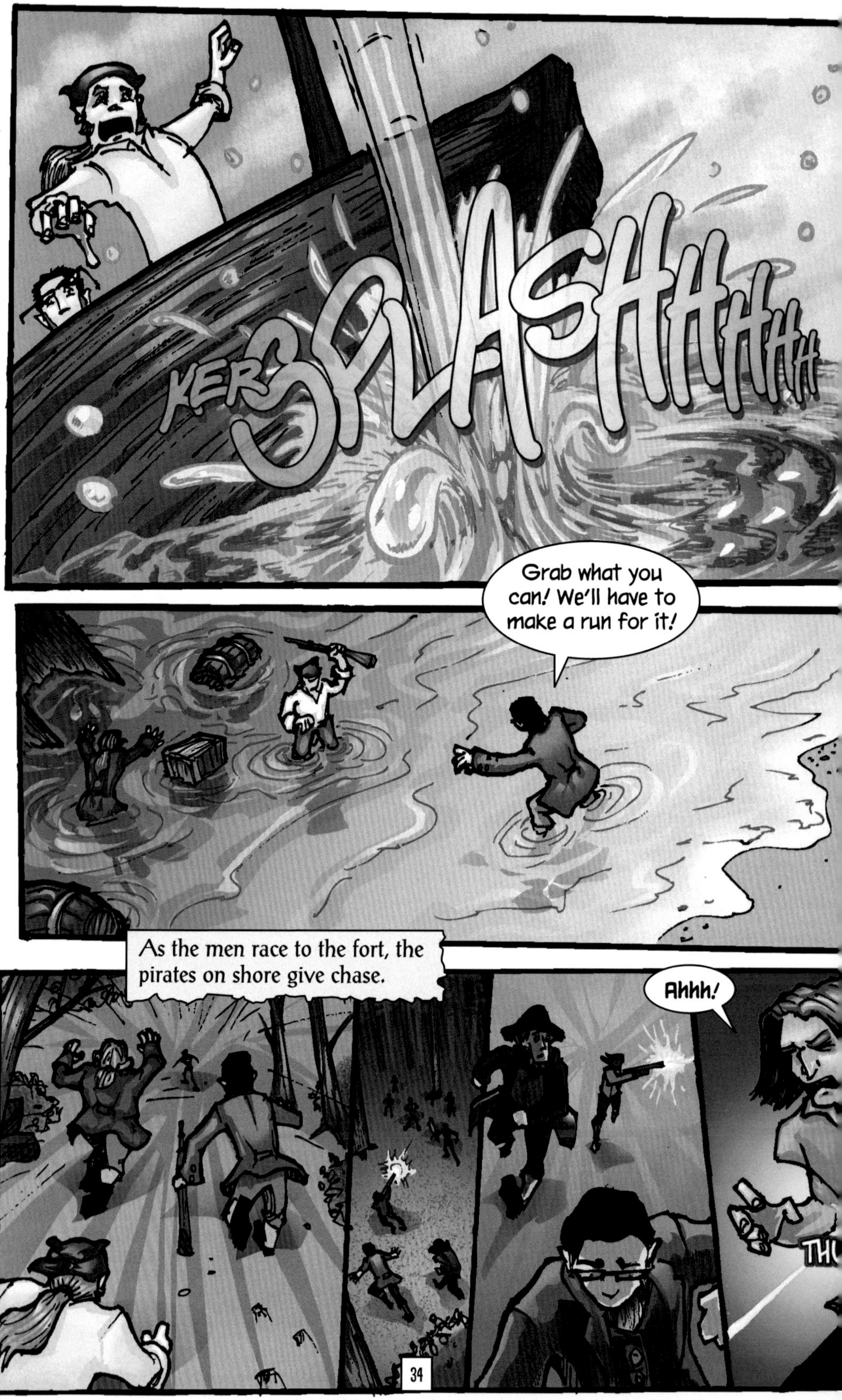

KERSPLASHHHHHHH
Grab what you can! We'll have to make a run for it!
As the men race to the fort, the pirates on shore give chase.
Ahhh!

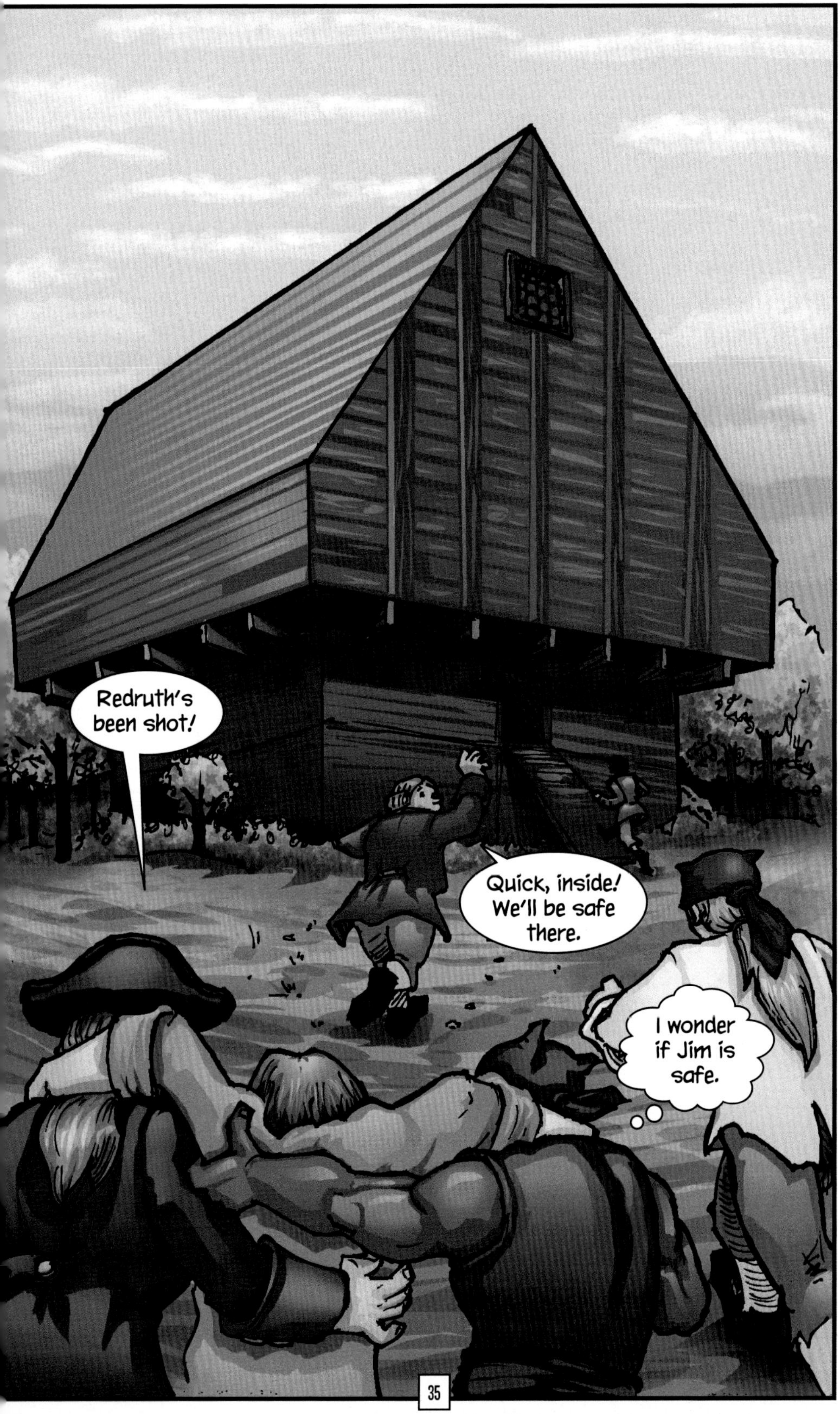
Redruth's been shot!
Quick, inside! We'll be safe there.
I wonder if Jim is safe.

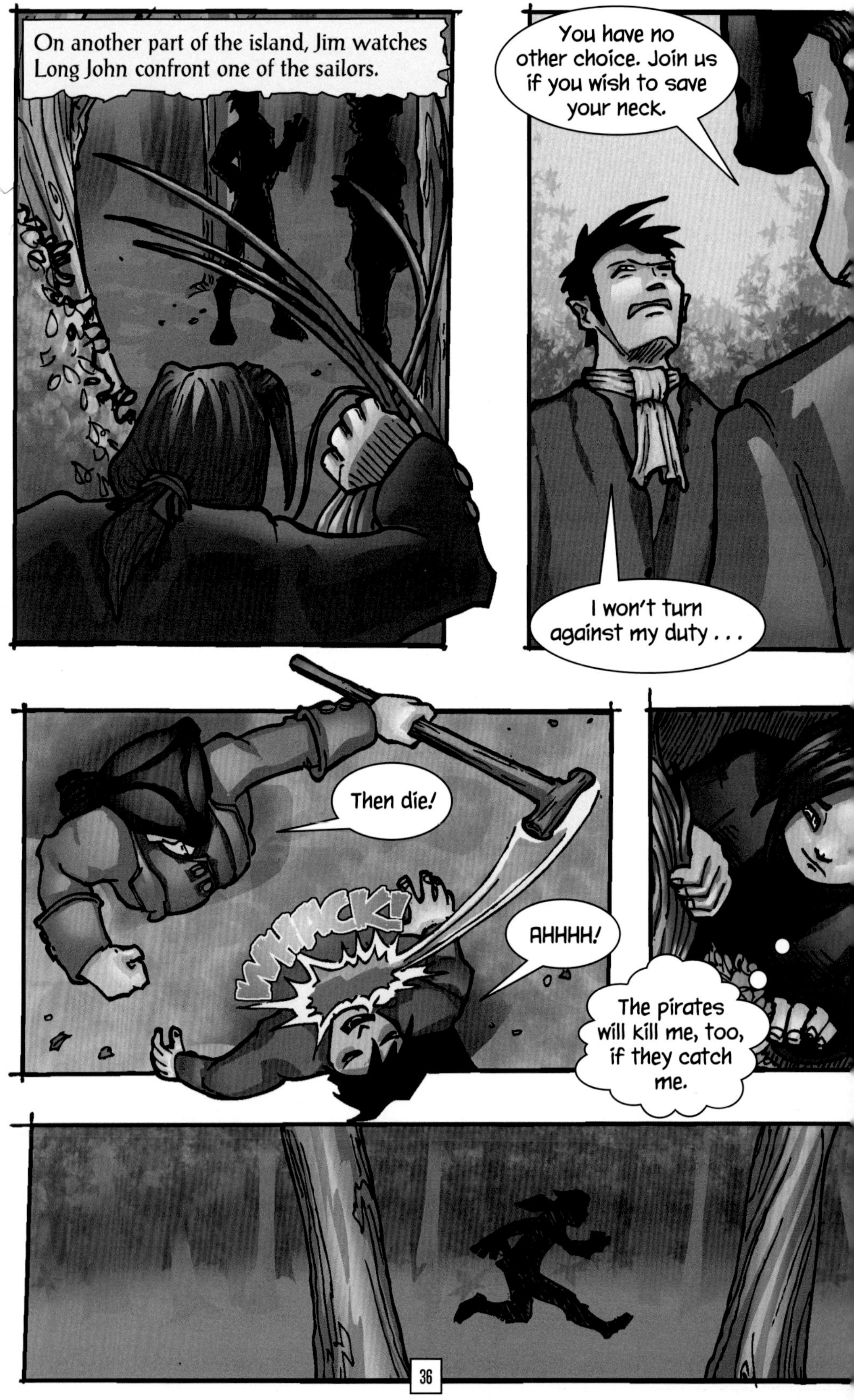
On another part of the island, Jim watches Long John confront one of the sailors.
You have no other choice. Join us if you wish to save your neck.
I won't turn against my duty . . .
Then die!
WHACK!
AHHHH!
The pirates will kill me, too, if they catch me.

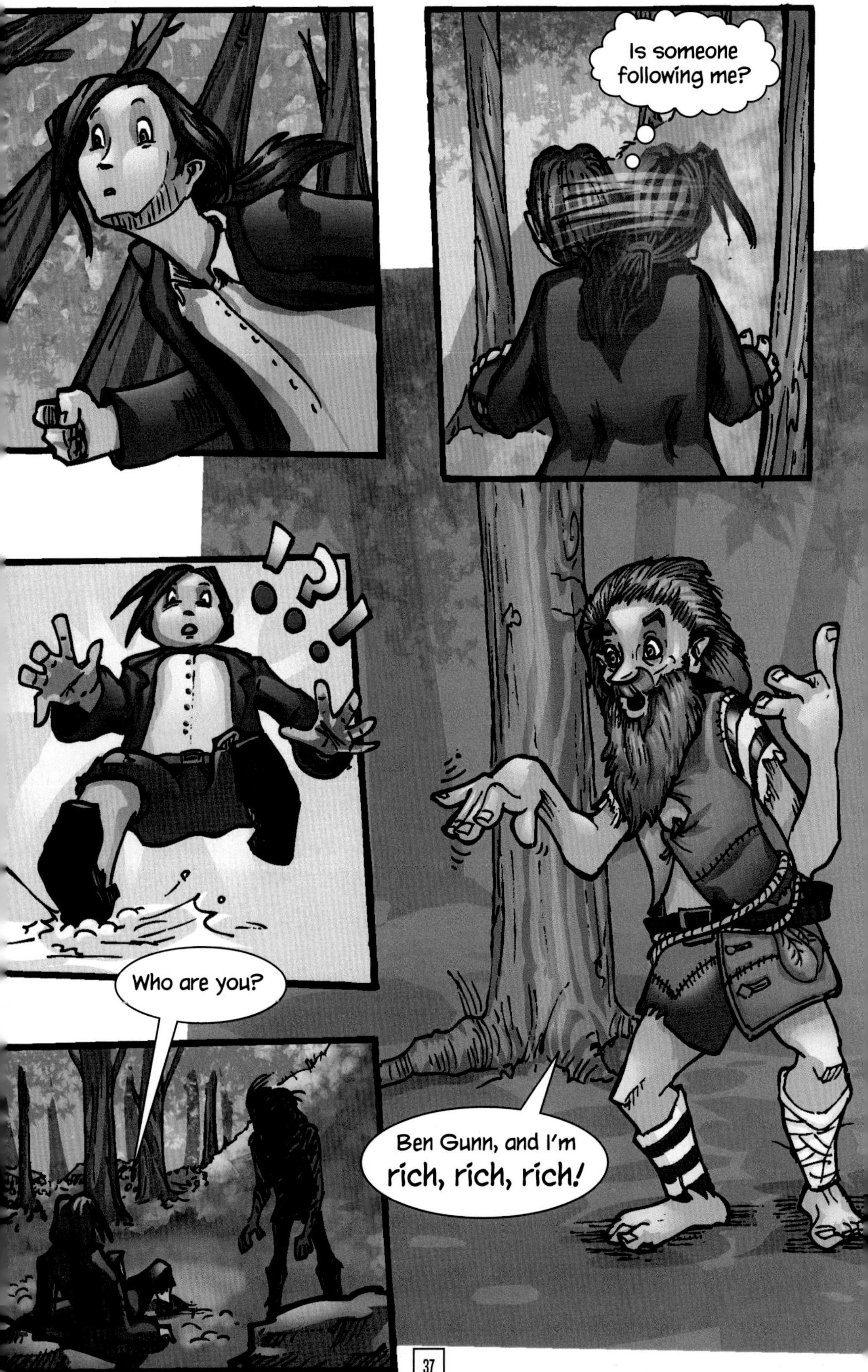
Is someone following me?
Who are you?
Ben Gunn, and I'm rich, rich, rich!

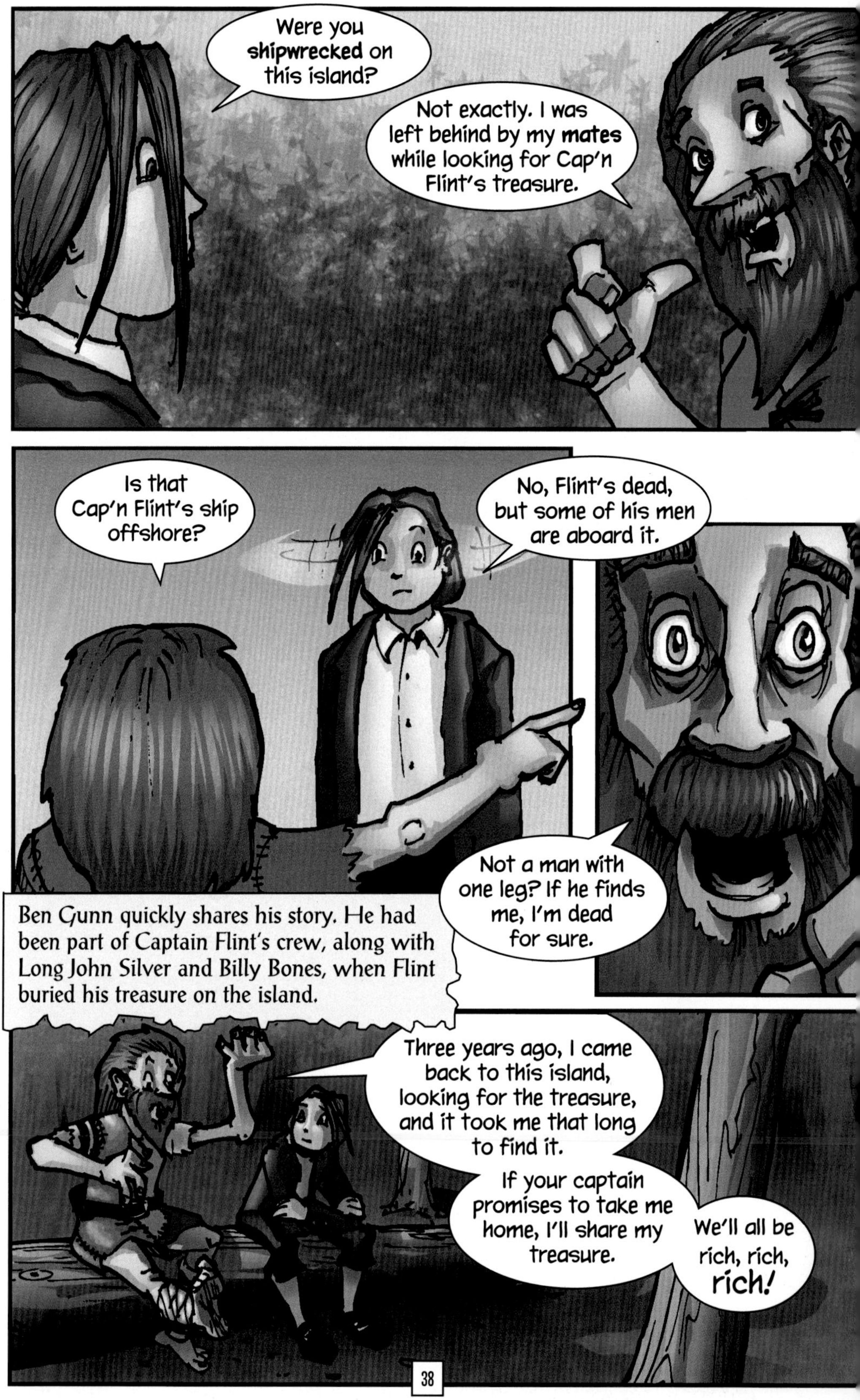
Were you shipwrecked on this island?
Not exactly. I was left behind by my mates while looking for Cap'n Flint's treasure.
Is that Cap'n Flint's ship offshore?
No, Flint's dead, but some of his men are aboard it.
Not a man with one leg? If he finds me, I'm dead for sure.
Ben Gunn quickly shares his story. He had been part of Captain Flint's crew, along with Long John Silver and Billy Bones, when Flint buried his treasure on the island.
Three years ago, I came back to this island, looking for the treasure, and it took me that long to find it.
If your captain promises to take me home, I'll share my treasure.
We'll all be rich, rich, rich!

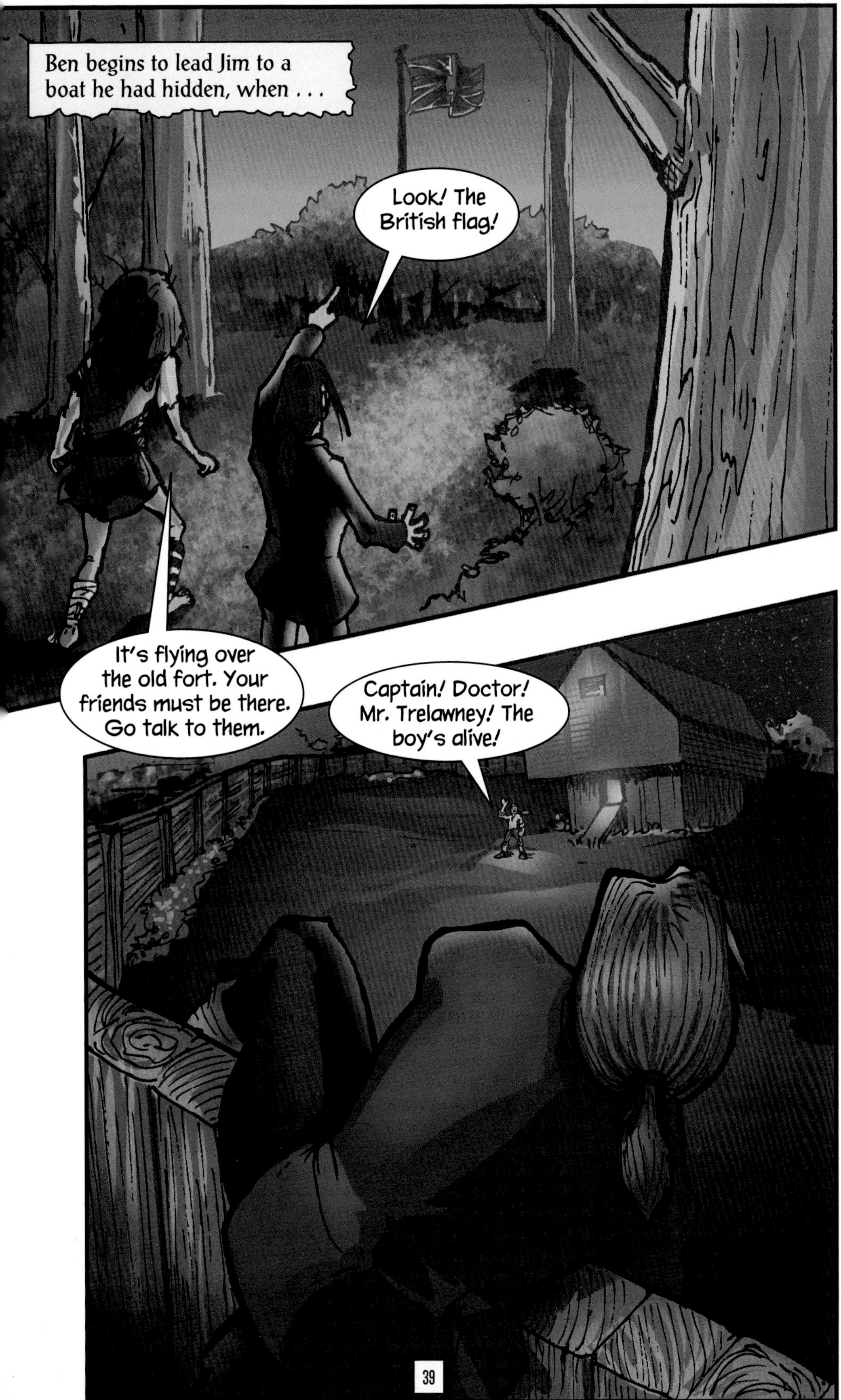

Ben begins to lead Jim to a boat he had hidden, when . . .
Look! The British flag!
It's flying over the old fort. Your friends must be there. Go talk to them.
Captain! Doctor! Mr. Trelawney! The boy's alive!

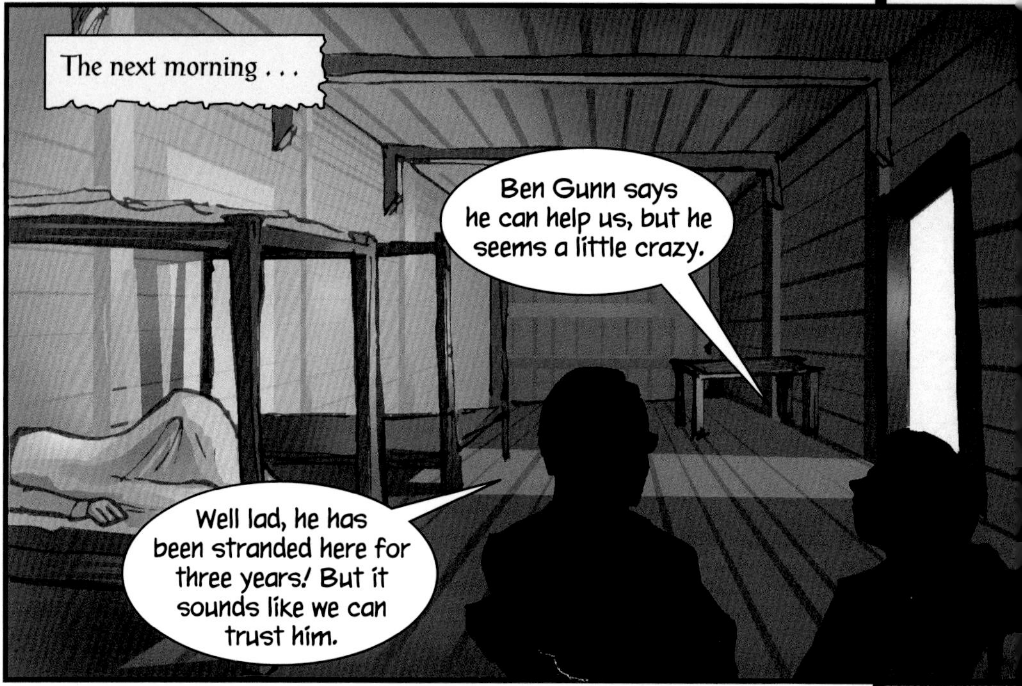
The next morning . . .
Ben Gunn says he can help us, but he seems a little crazy.
Well lad, he has been stranded here for three years! But it sounds like we can trust him.

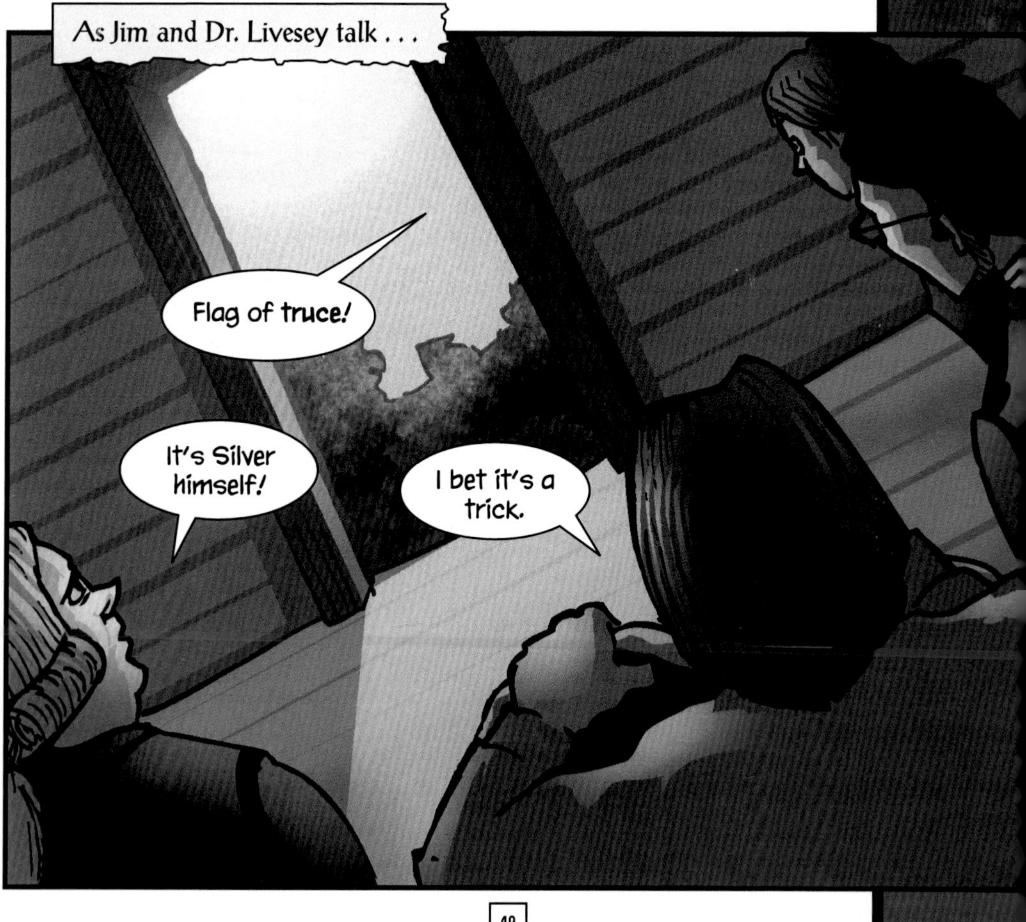
As Jim and Dr. Livesey talk . . .
Flag of truce!
It's Silver himself!
I bet it's a trick.

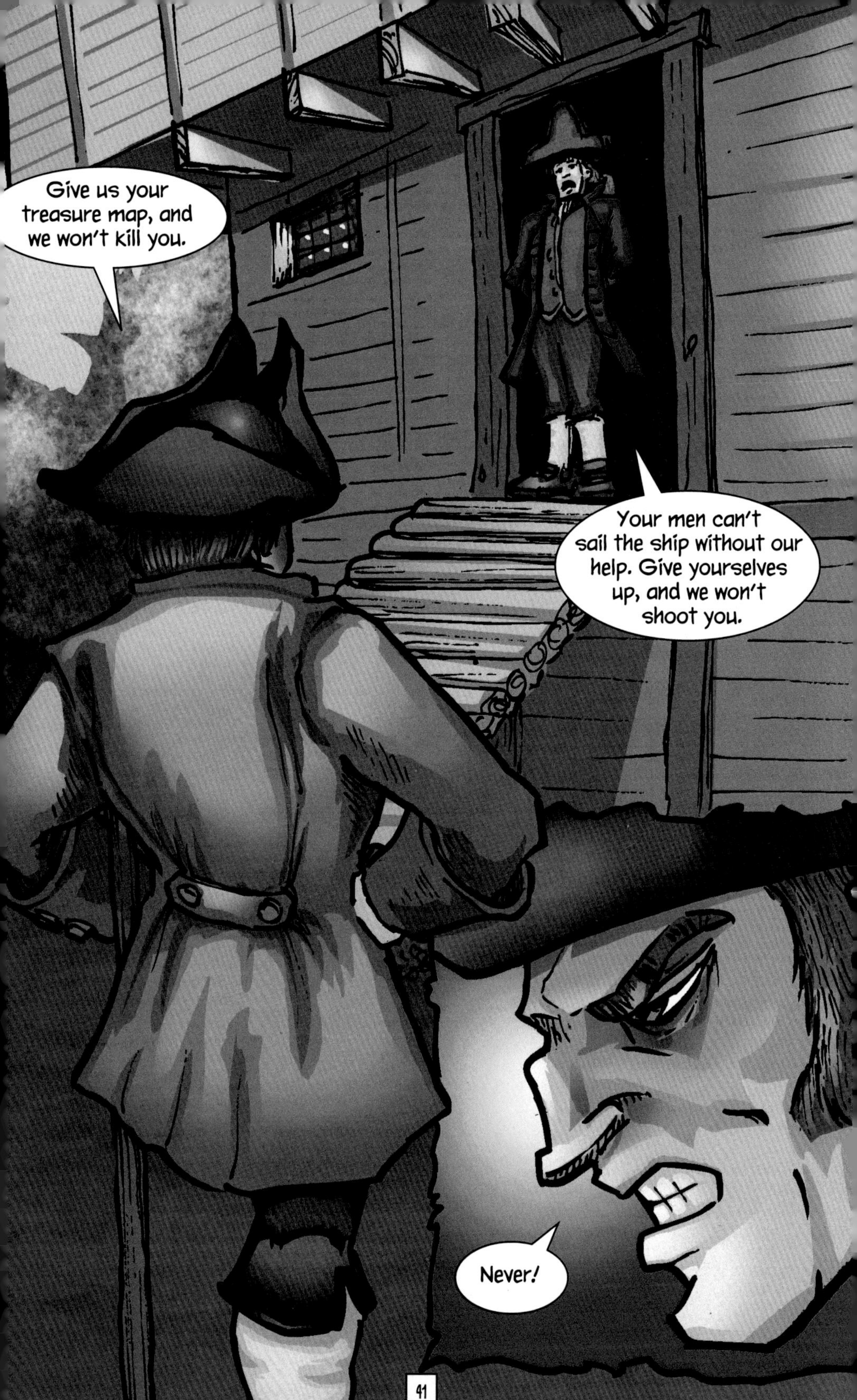
Give us your treasure map, and we won't kill you.
Your men can't sail the ship without our help. Give yourselves up, and we won't shoot you.
Never!

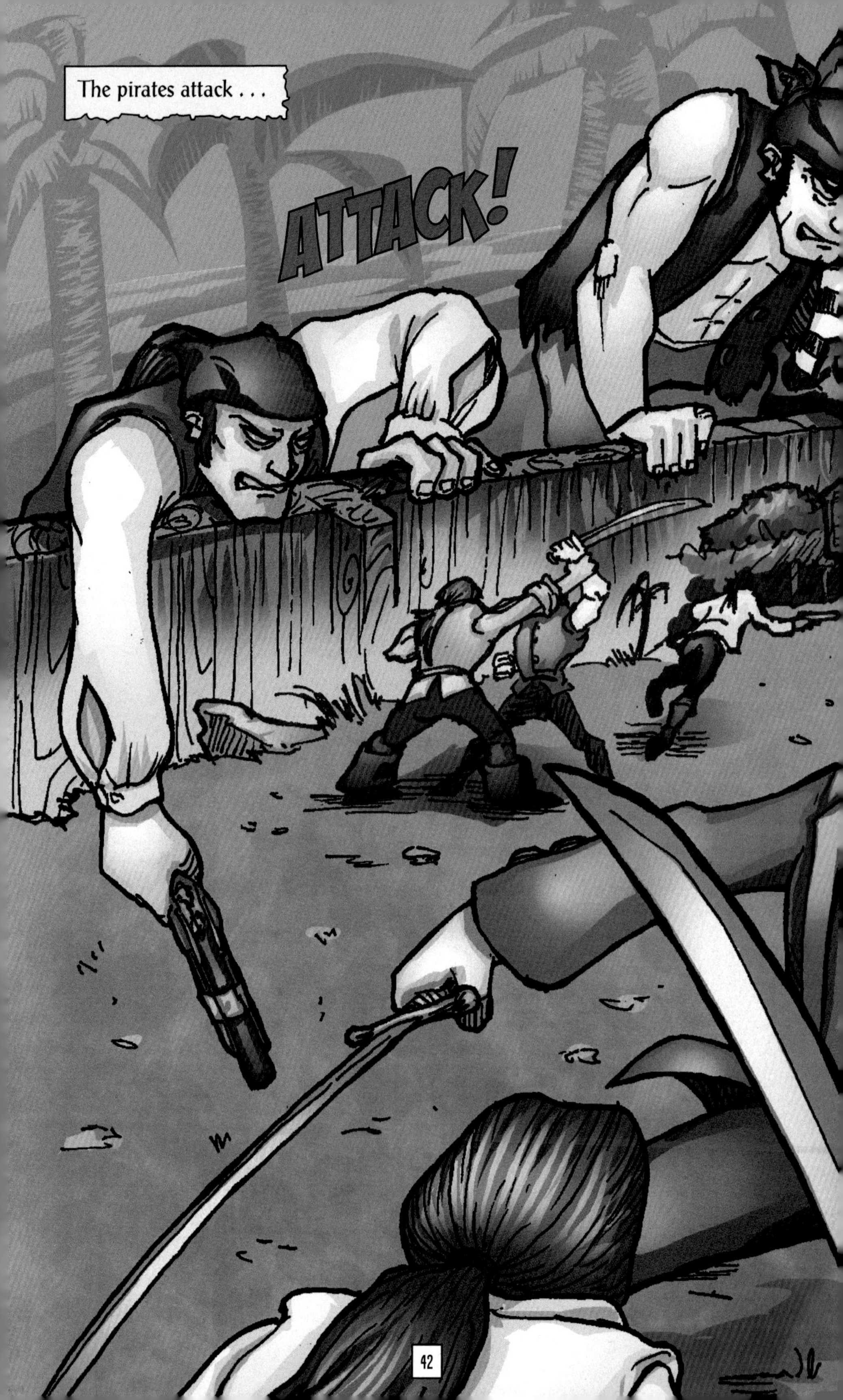
The pirates attack . . .
ATTACK!

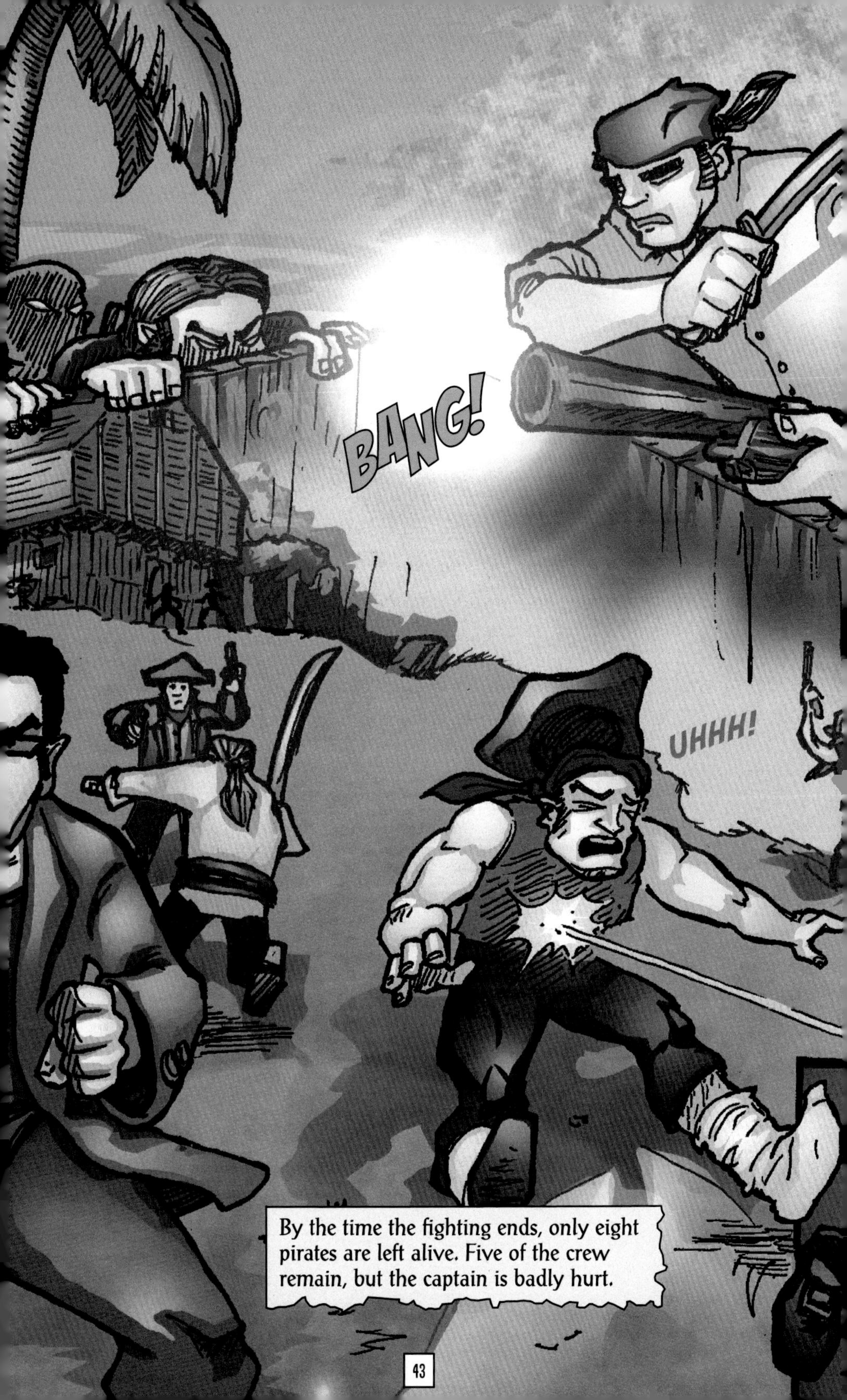
BANG!
UHHH!
By the time the fighting ends, only eight pirates are left alive. Five of the crew remain, but the captain is badly hurt.

CHAPTER 4 Jim's Sea Adventure

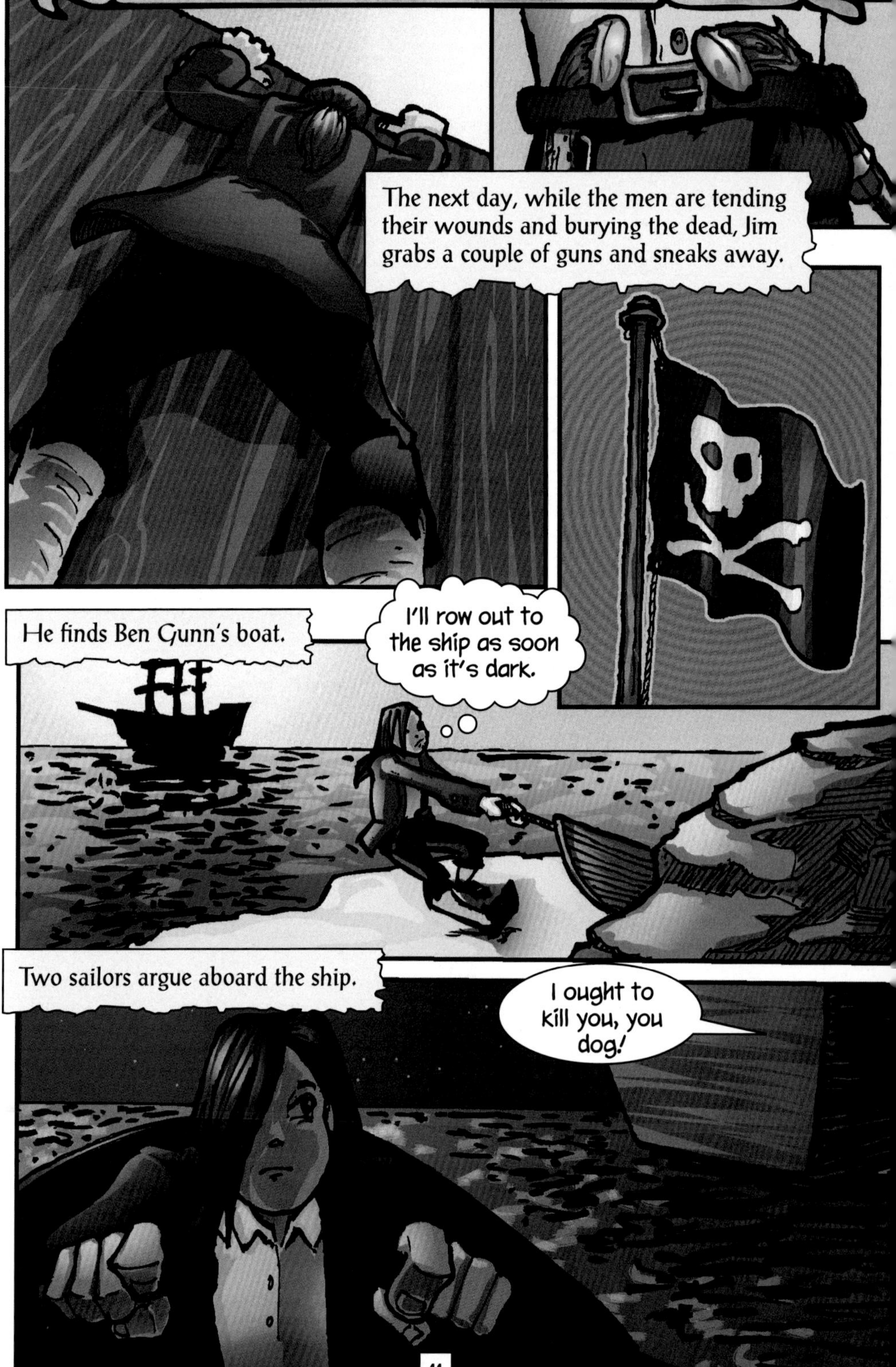

The next day, while the men are tending their wounds and burying the dead, Jim grabs a couple of guns and sneaks away.
He finds Ben Gunn's boat.
I'll row out to the ship as soon as it's dark.
Two sailors argue aboard the ship.
I ought to kill you, you dog!

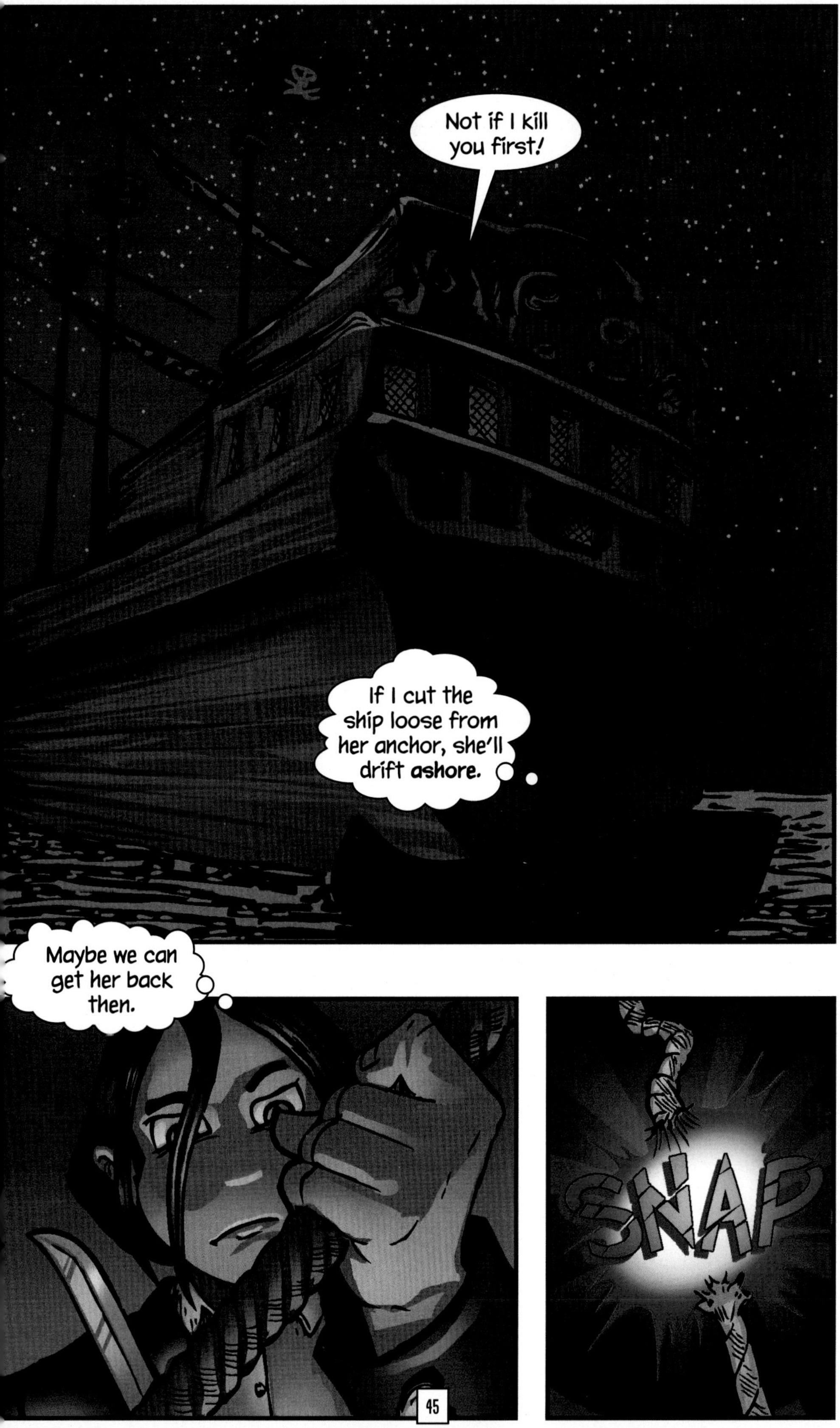
Not if I kill you first!
If I cut the ship loose from her anchor, she'll drift **ashore.**
Maybe we can get her back then.
SNAP

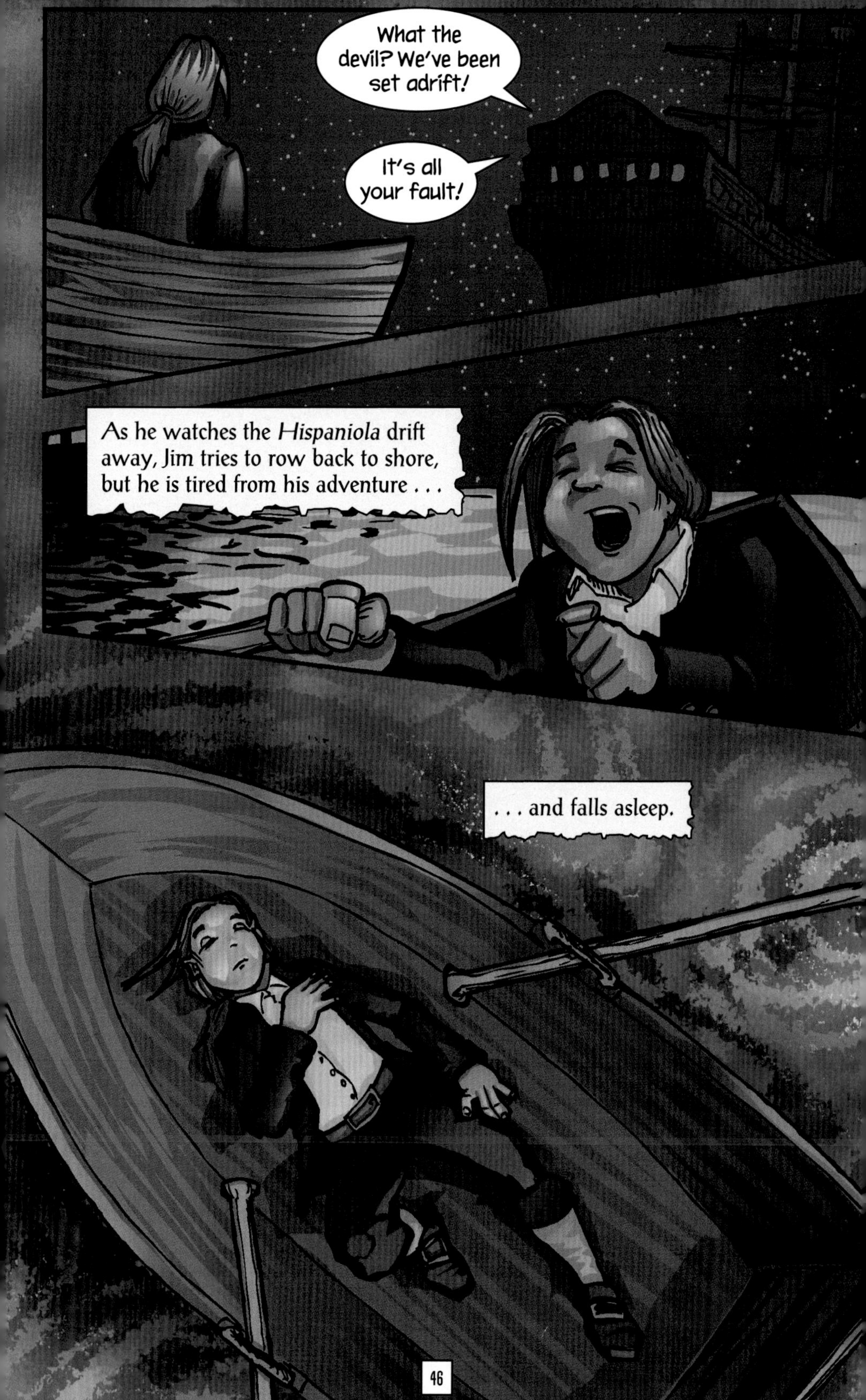
What the devil? We've been set adrift!
It's all your fault!
As he watches the *Hispaniola* drift away, Jim tries to row back to shore, but he is tired from his adventure . . .
. . . and falls asleep.

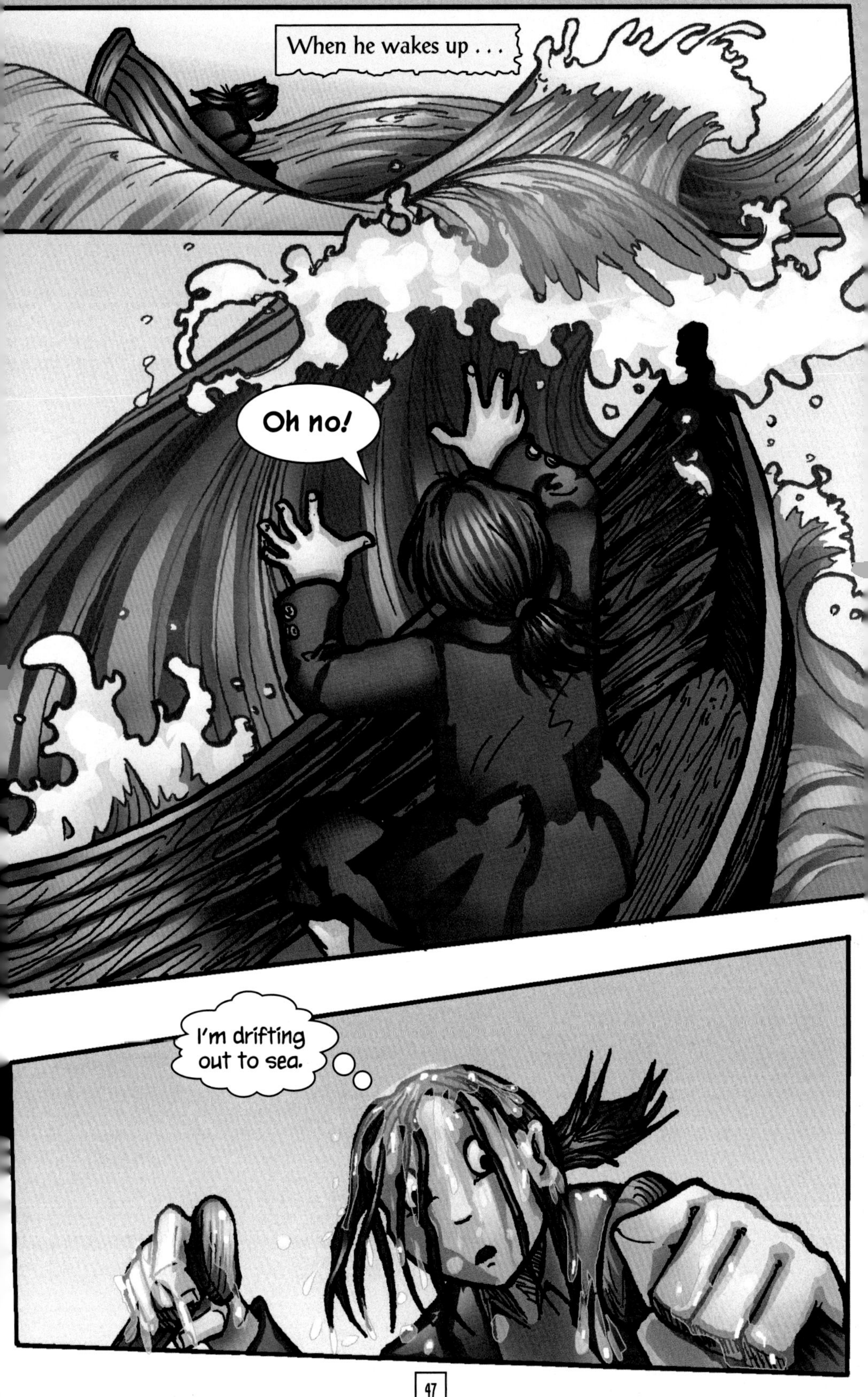
When he wakes up . . .
Oh no!
I'm drifting out to sea.

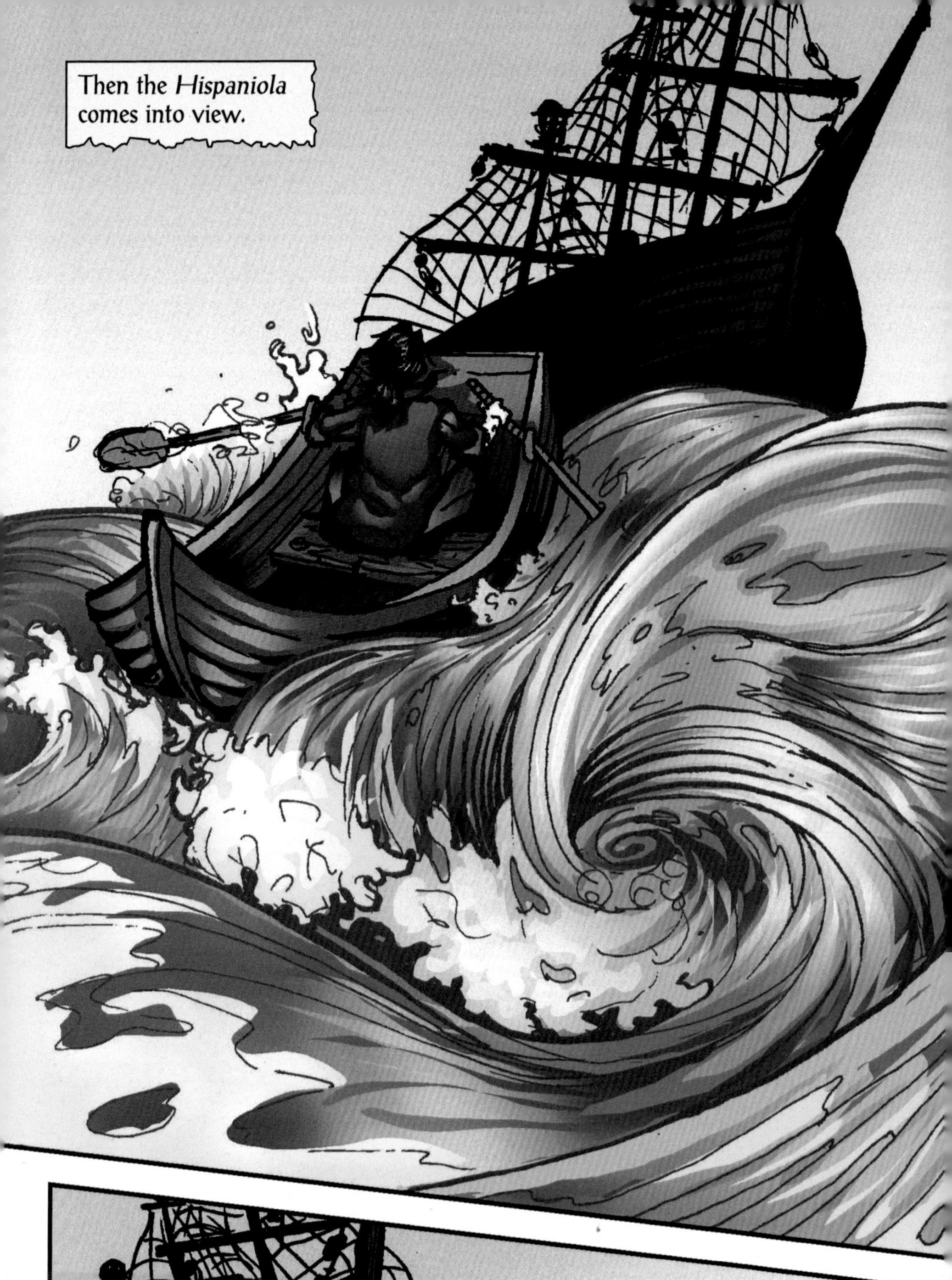
Then the *Hispaniola* comes into view.

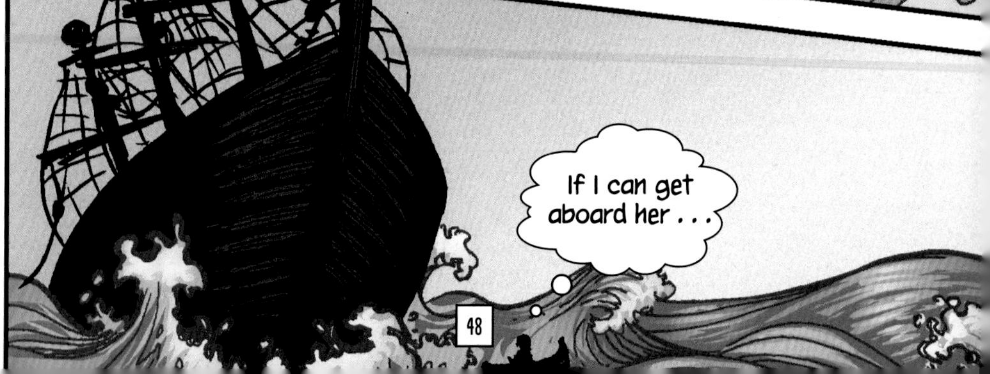
If I can get aboard her . . .

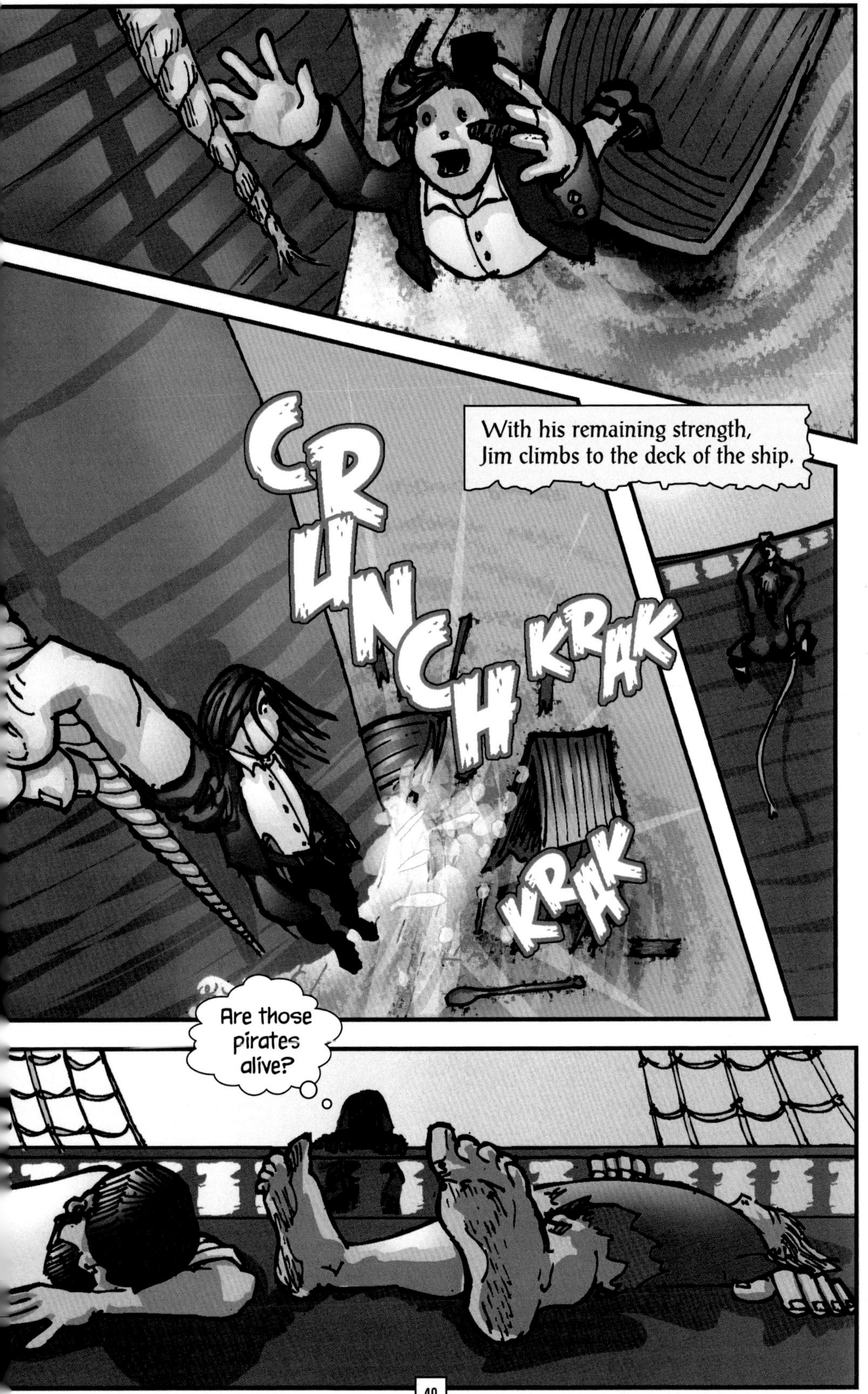
With his remaining strength, Jim climbs to the deck of the ship.
CRUNCH
KRAK
KRAK
Are those pirates alive?

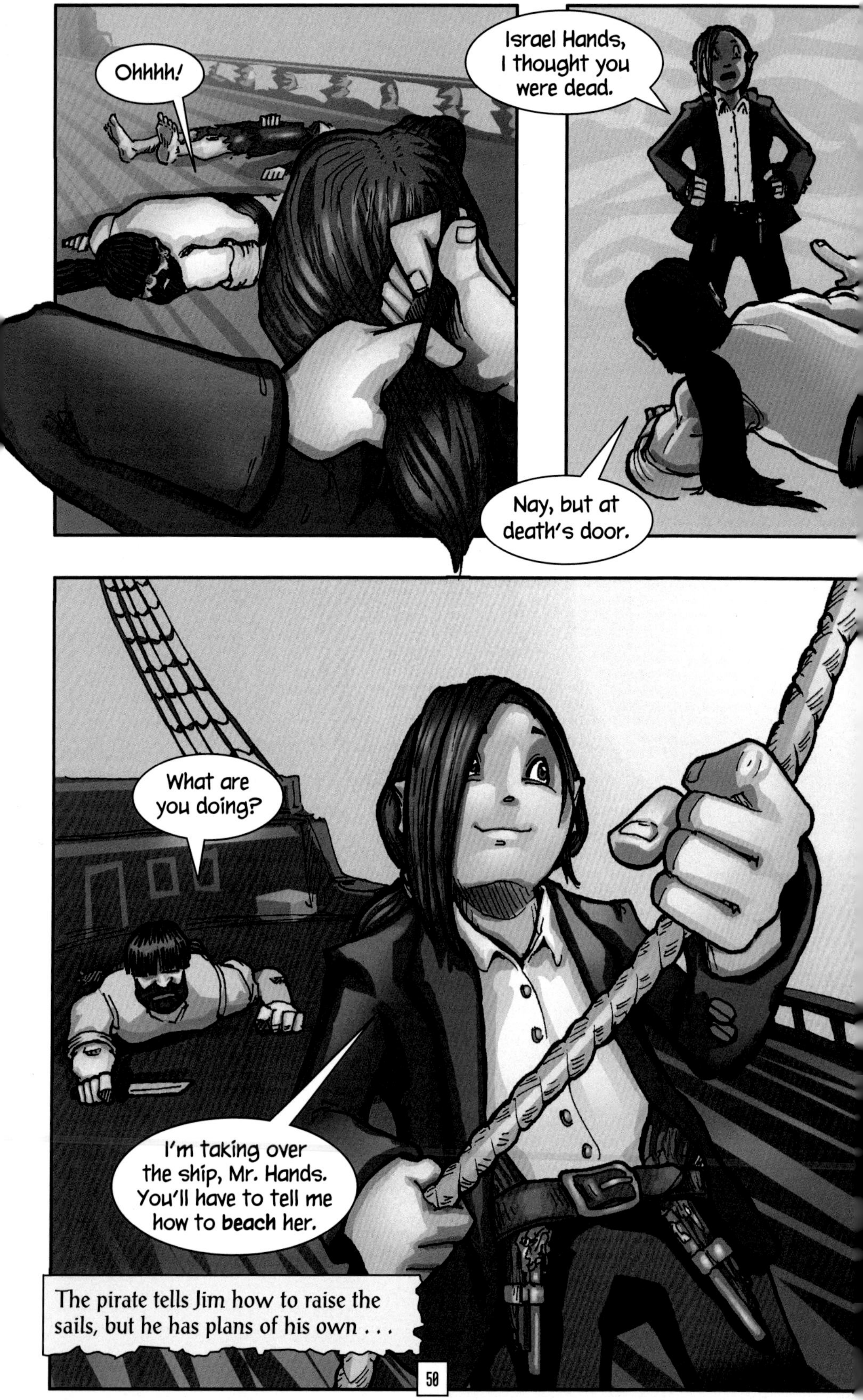

Ohhhh!
Israel Hands, I thought you were dead.
Nay, but at death's door.
What are you doing?
I'm taking over the ship, Mr. Hands. You'll have to tell me how to **beach** her.
The pirate tells Jim how to raise the sails, but he has plans of his own . . .

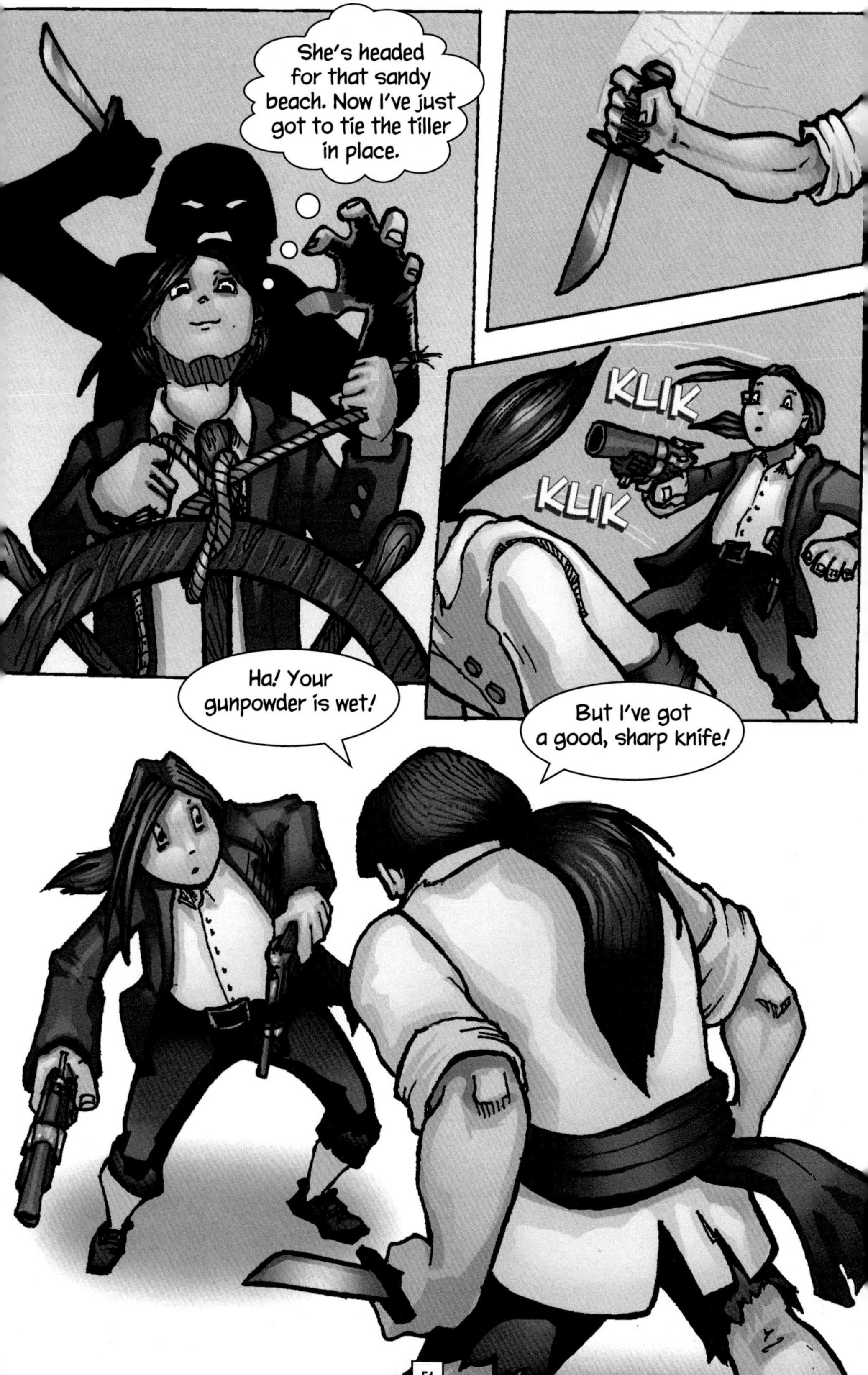
She's headed for that sandy beach. Now I've just got to tie the tiller in place.
KLIK
KLIK
Ha! Your gunpowder is wet!
But I've got a good, sharp knife!

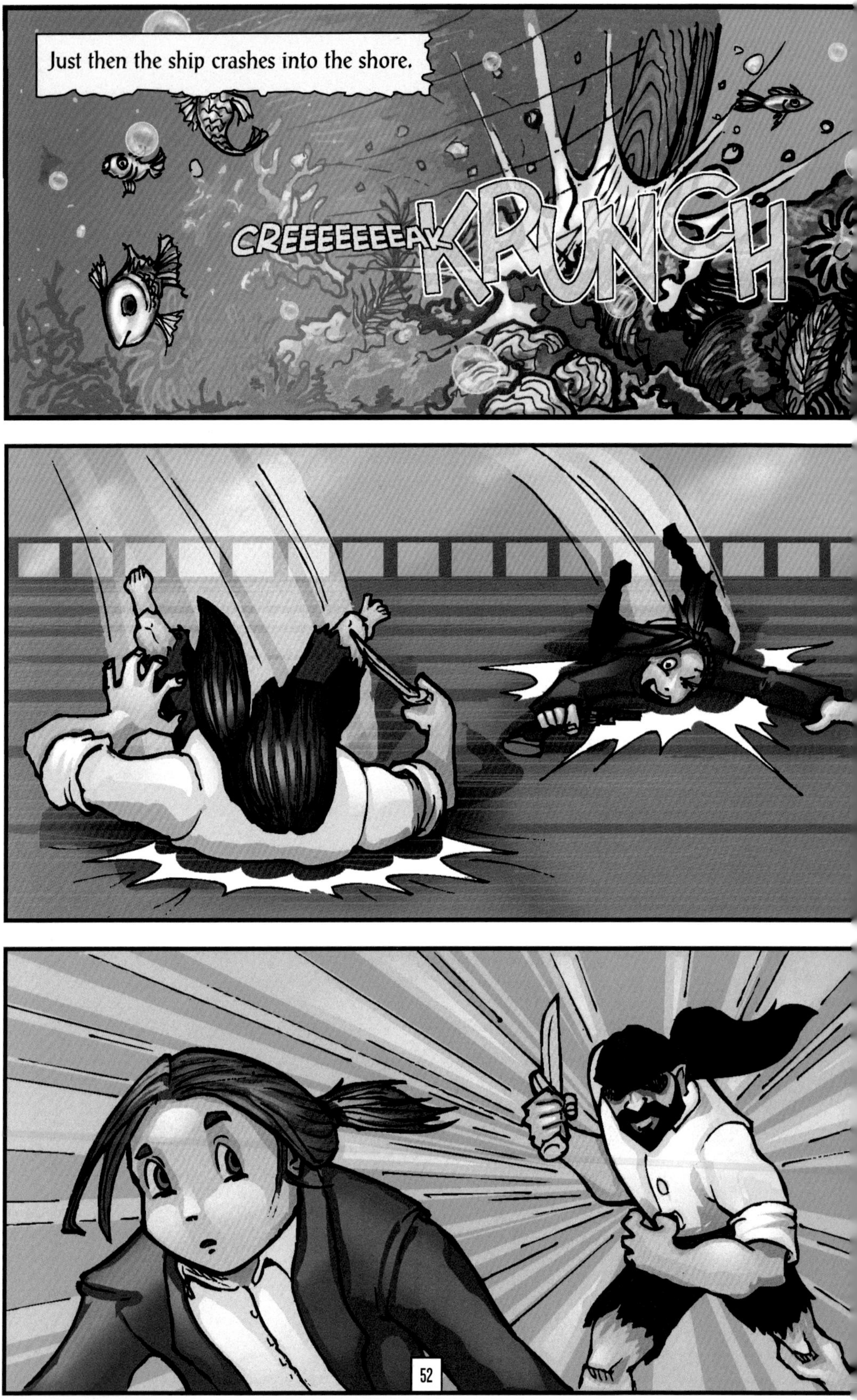
Just then the ship crashes into the shore.
CREEEEEEEEAK
KRUNCH

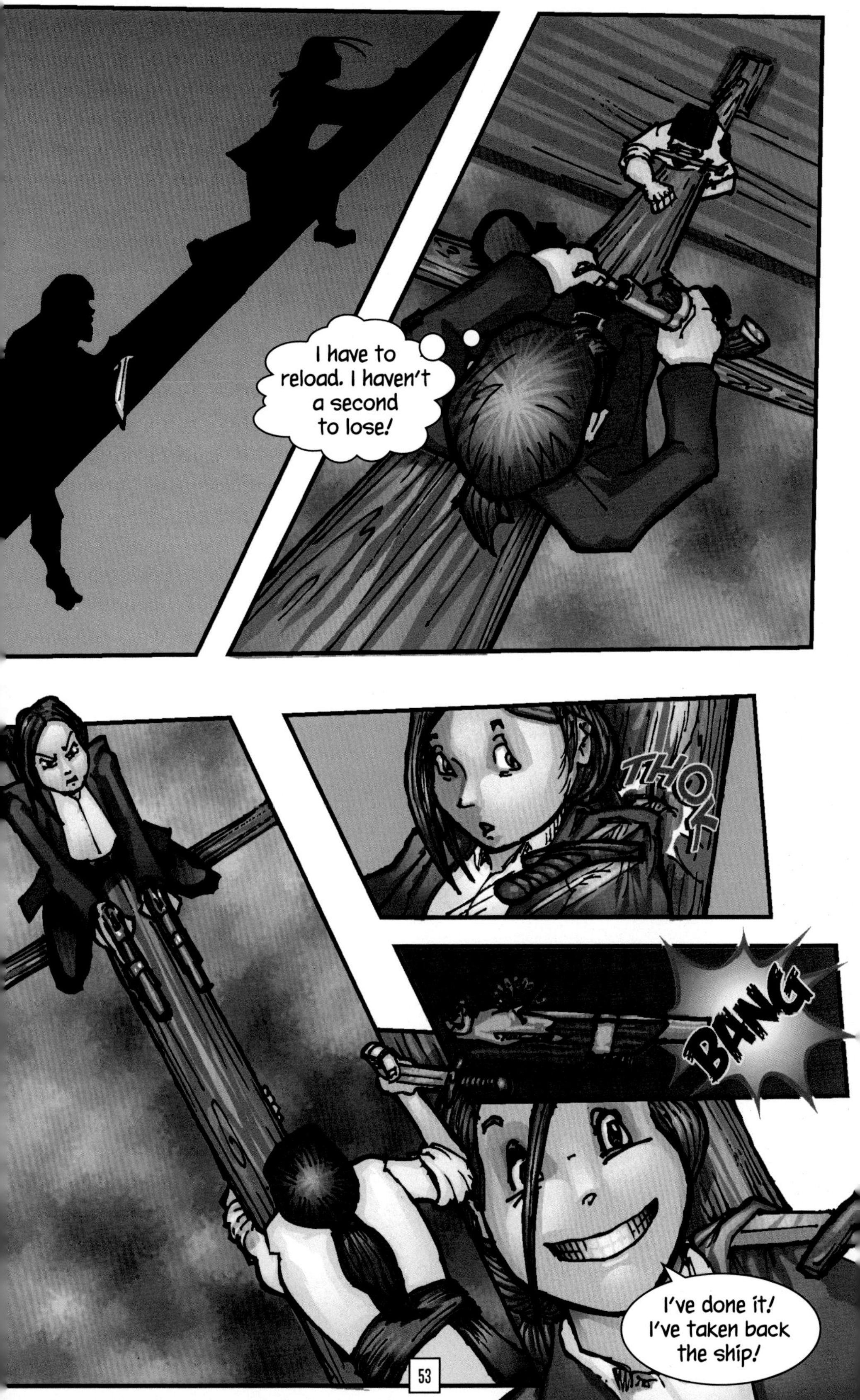
I have to reload. I haven't a second to lose!
THOK
BANG
I've done it! I've taken back the ship!

CHAPTER 5 Captain Silver

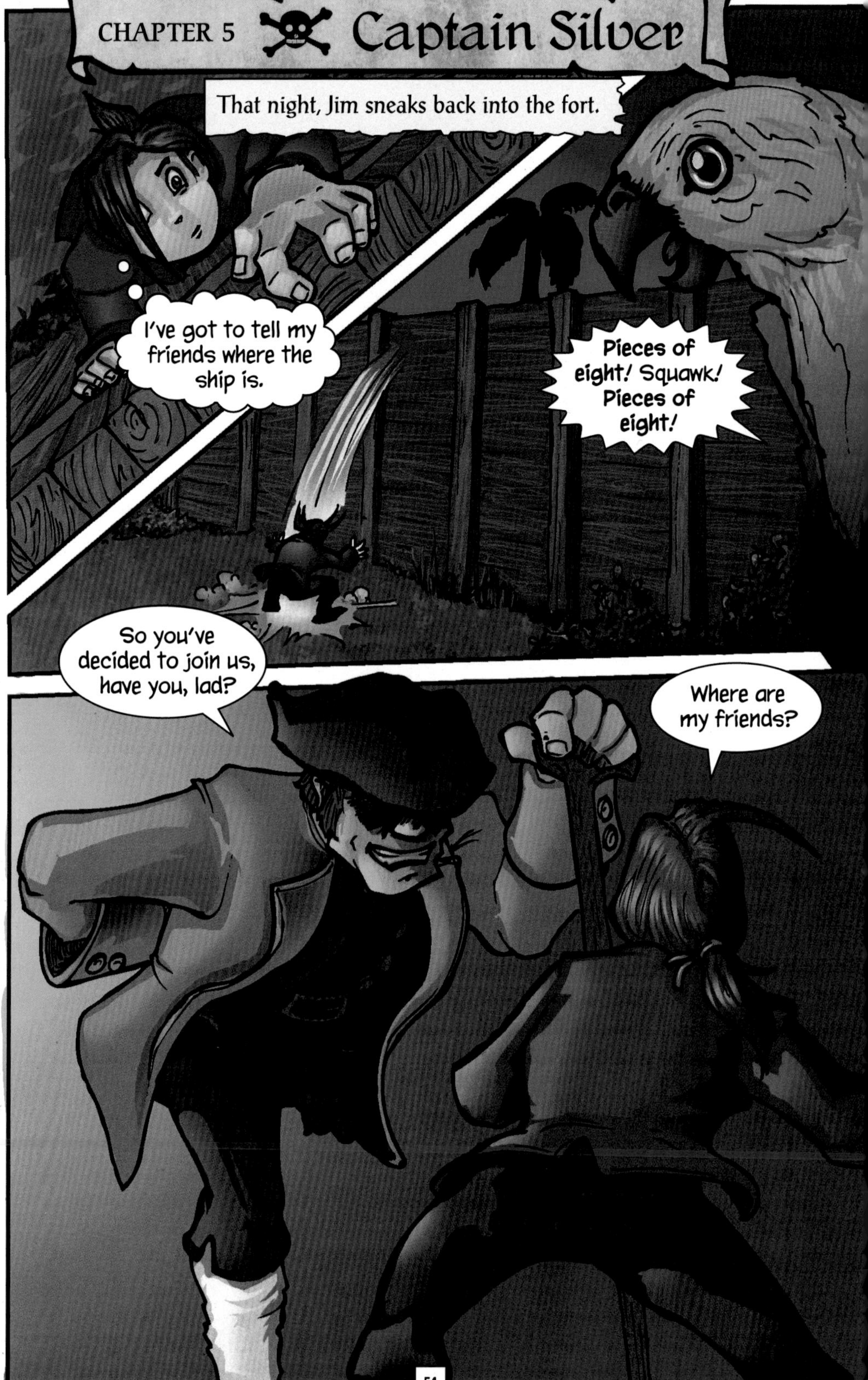
That night, Jim sneaks back into the fort.
I've got to tell my friends where the ship is.
Pieces of eight! Squawk! Pieces of eight!
So you've decided to join us, have you, lad?
Where are my friends?

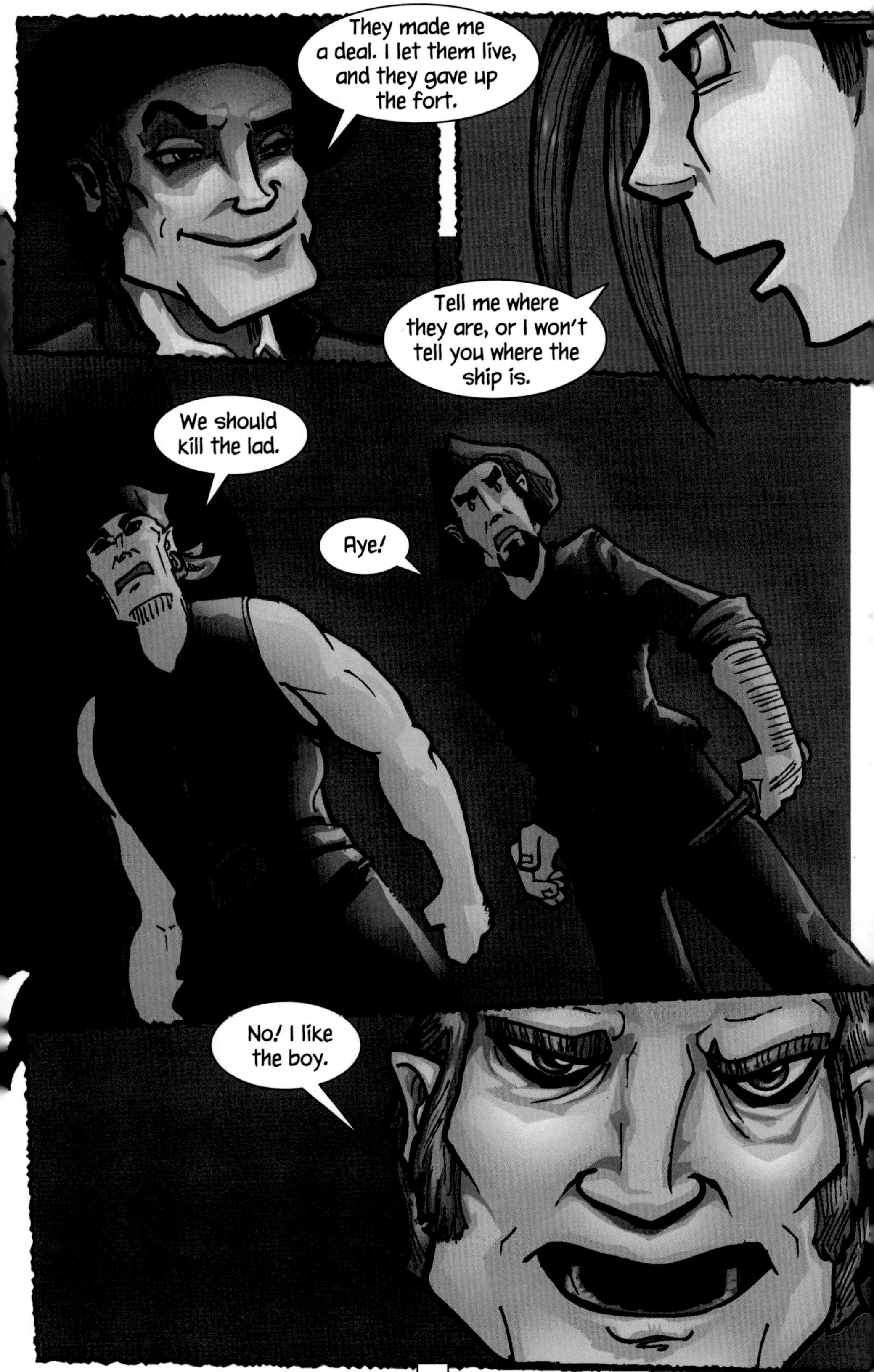
They made me a deal. I let them live, and they gave up the fort.
Tell me where they are, or I won't tell you where the ship is.
We should kill the lad.
Aye!
No! I like the boy.

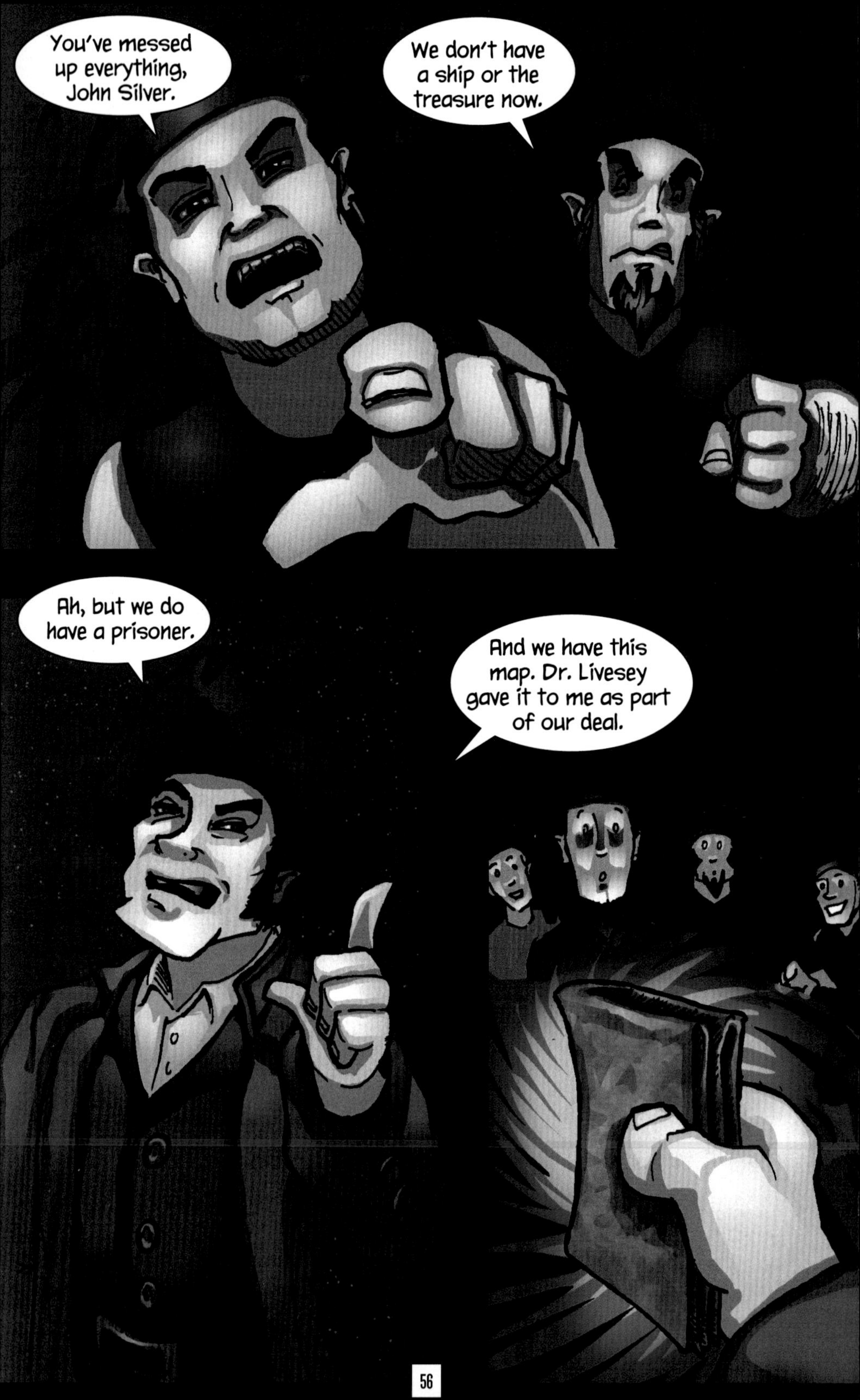
You've messed up everything, John Silver.
We don't have a ship or the treasure now.
Ah, but we do have a prisoner.
And we have this map. Dr. Livesey gave it to me as part of our deal.

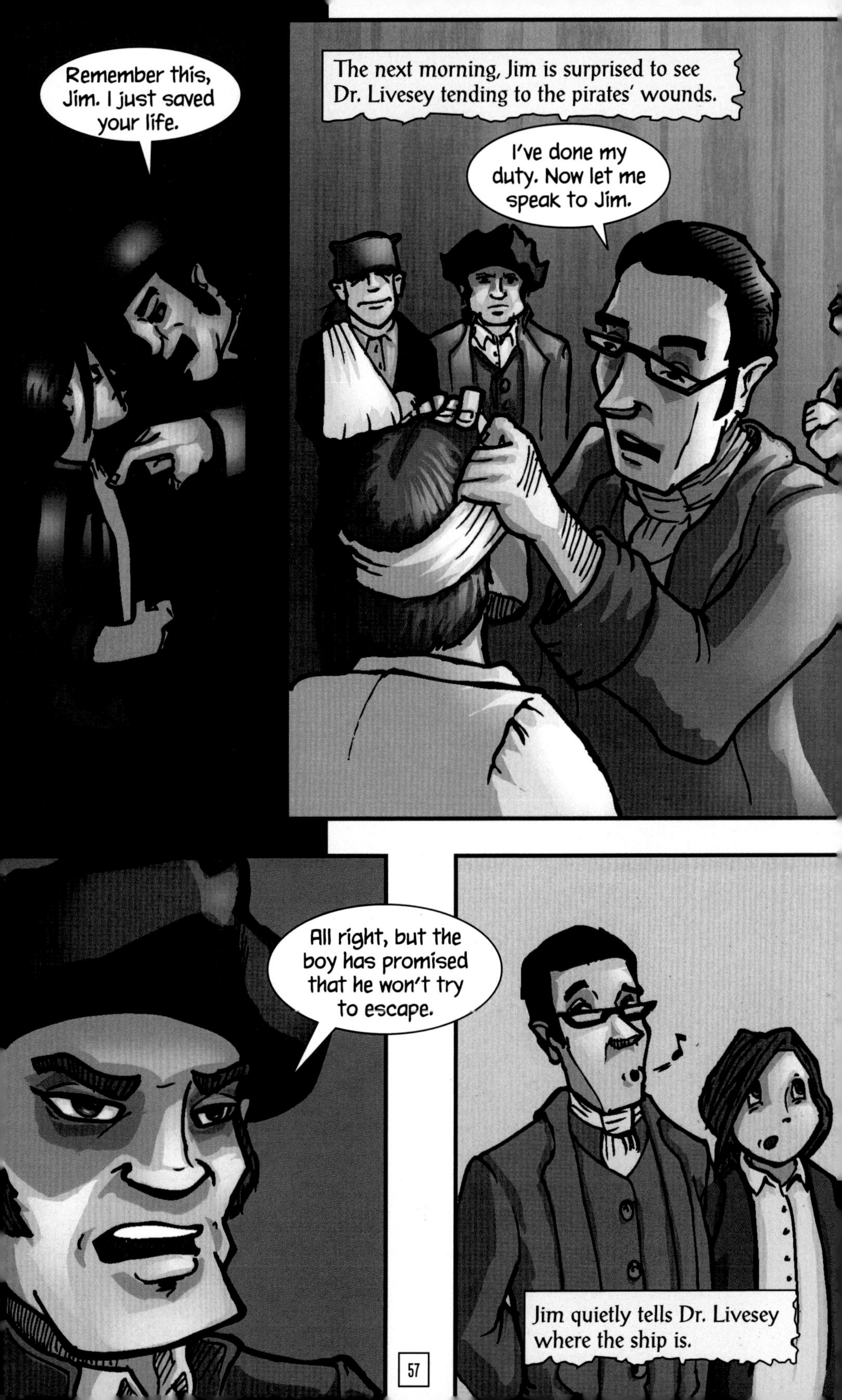

Remember this, Jim. I just saved your life.
The next morning, Jim is surprised to see Dr. Livesey tending to the pirates' wounds.
I've done my duty. Now let me speak to Jim.
All right, but the boy has promised that he won't try to escape.
Jim quietly tells Dr. Livesey where the ship is.

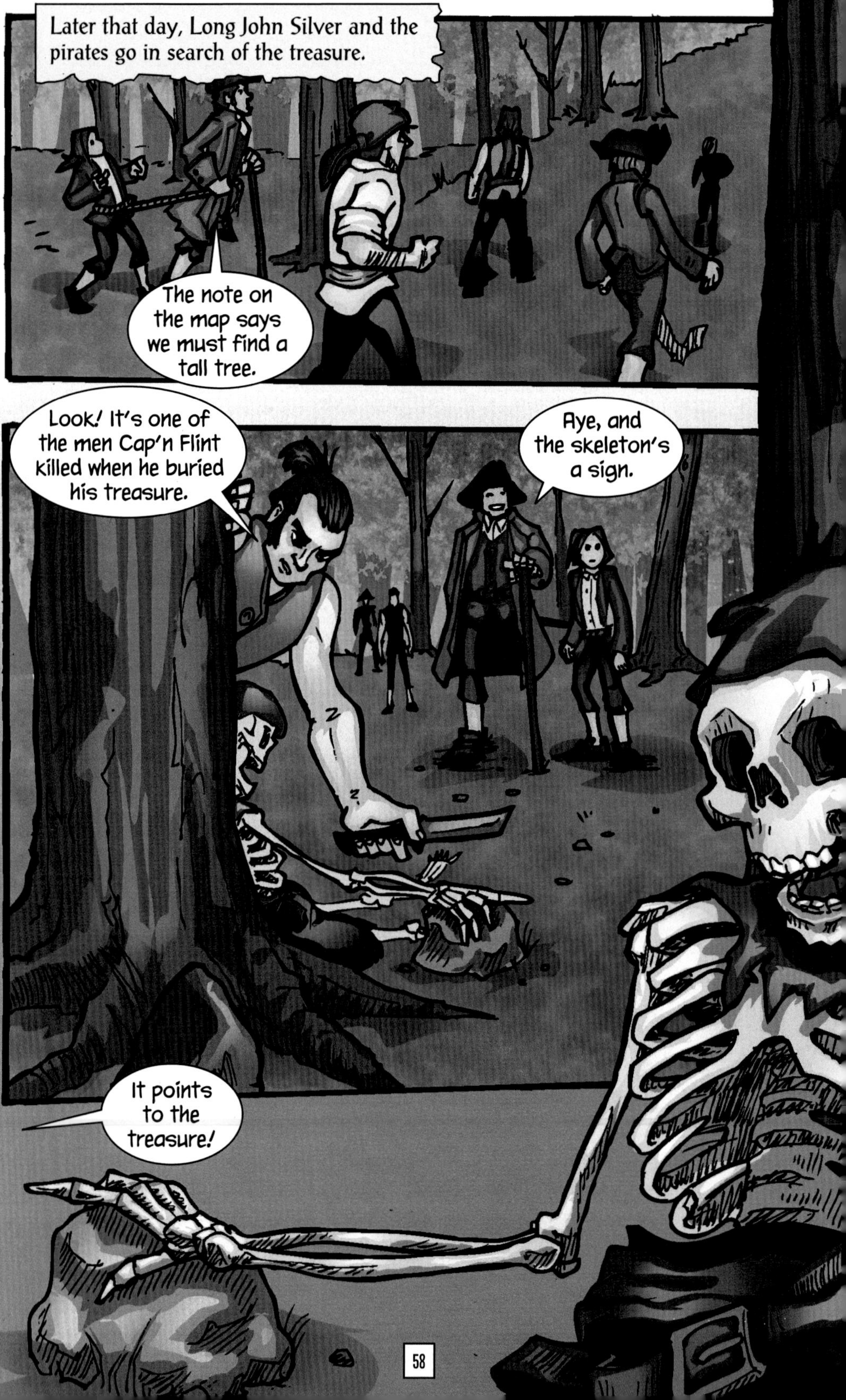

Later that day, Long John Silver and the pirates go in search of the treasure.
The note on the map says we must find a tall tree.
Look! It's one of the men Cap'n Flint killed when he buried his treasure.
Aye, and the skeleton's a sign.
It points to the treasure!

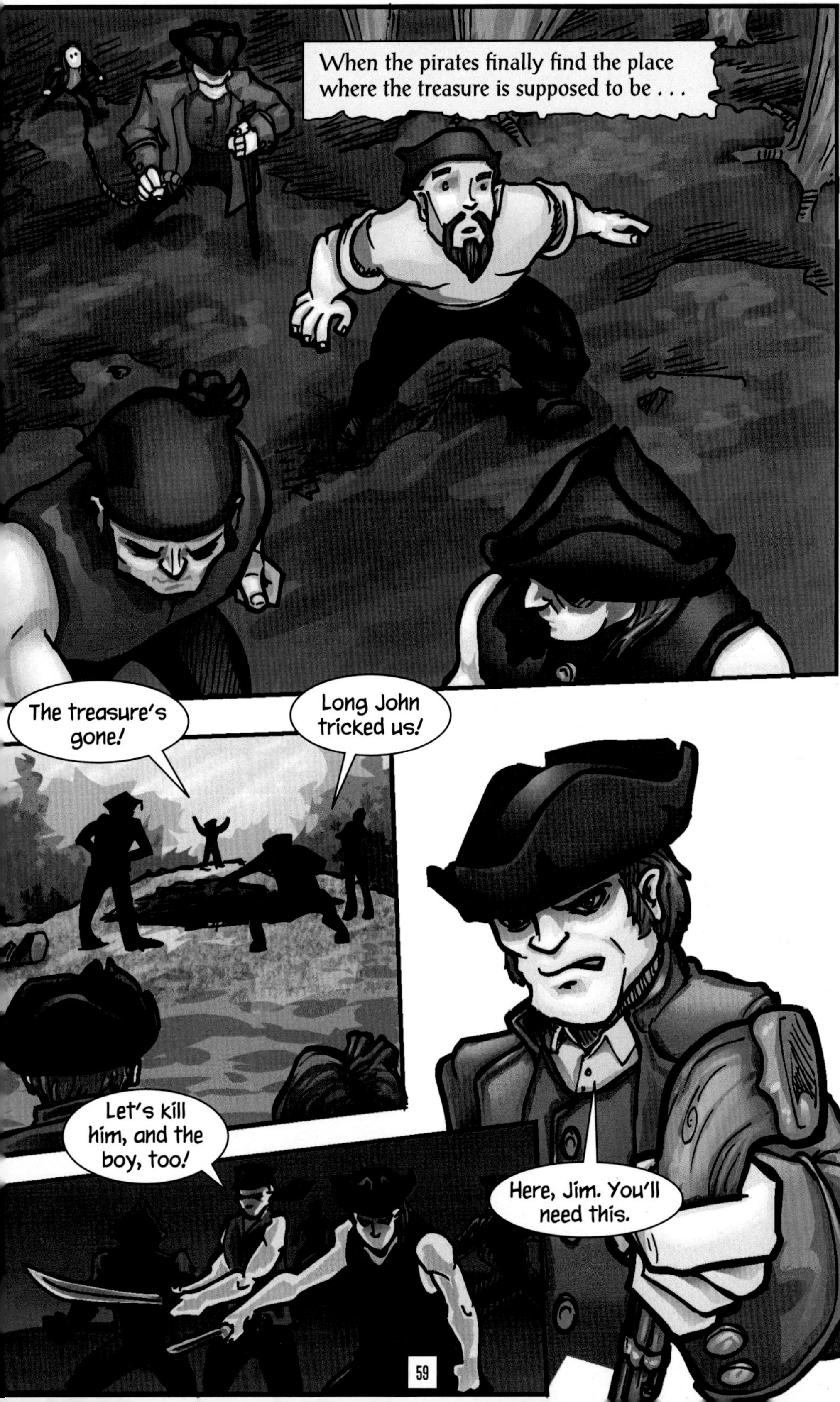

When the pirates finally find the place where the treasure is supposed to be . . .
The treasure's gone!
Long John tricked us!
Let's kill him, and the boy, too!
Here, Jim. You'll need this.

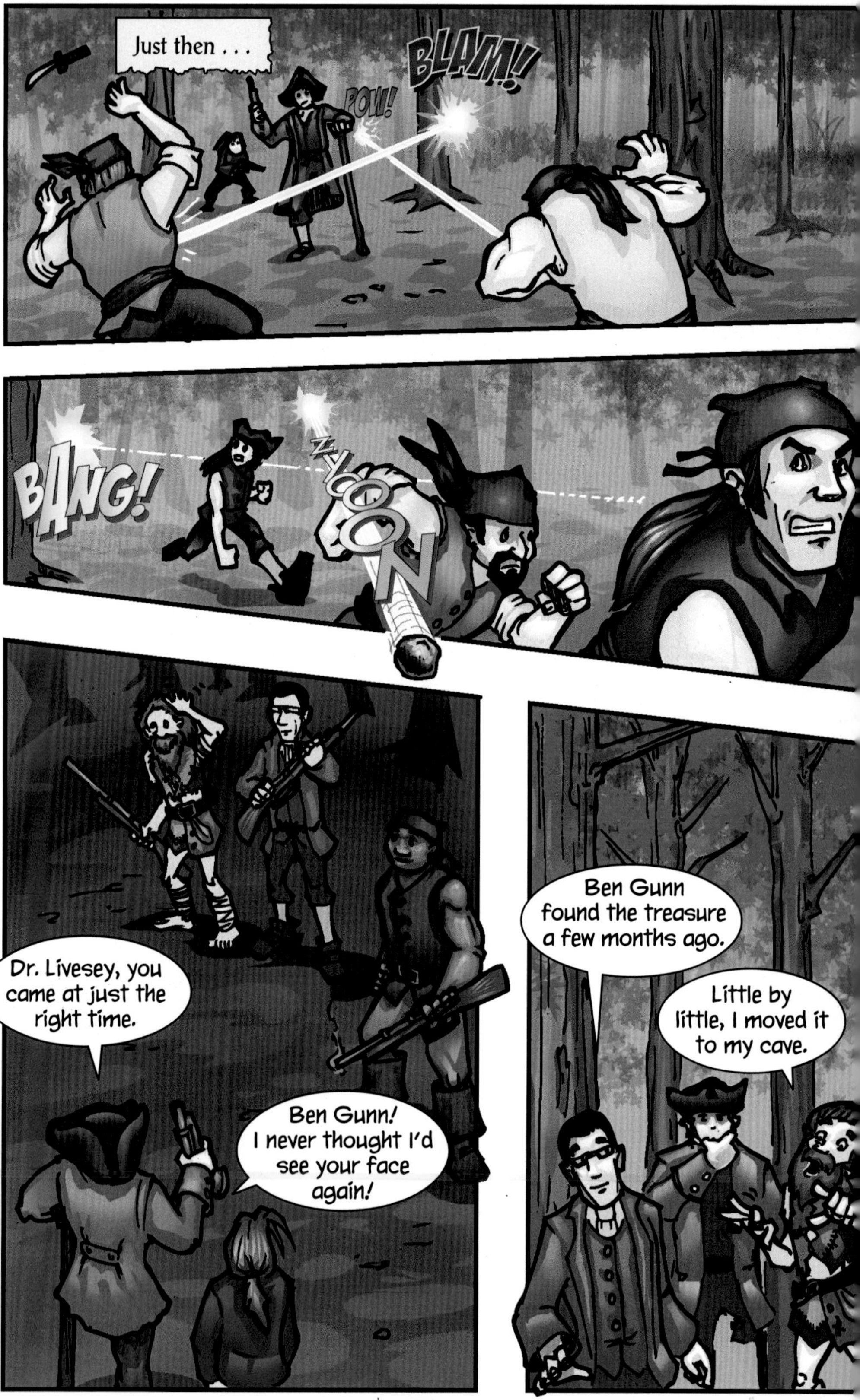
Just then . . .
BLAM!!
POW!
BANG!
ZYCOON
Dr. Livesey, you came at just the right time.
Ben Gunn! I never thought I'd see your face again!
Ben Gunn found the treasure a few months ago.
Little by little, I moved it to my cave.

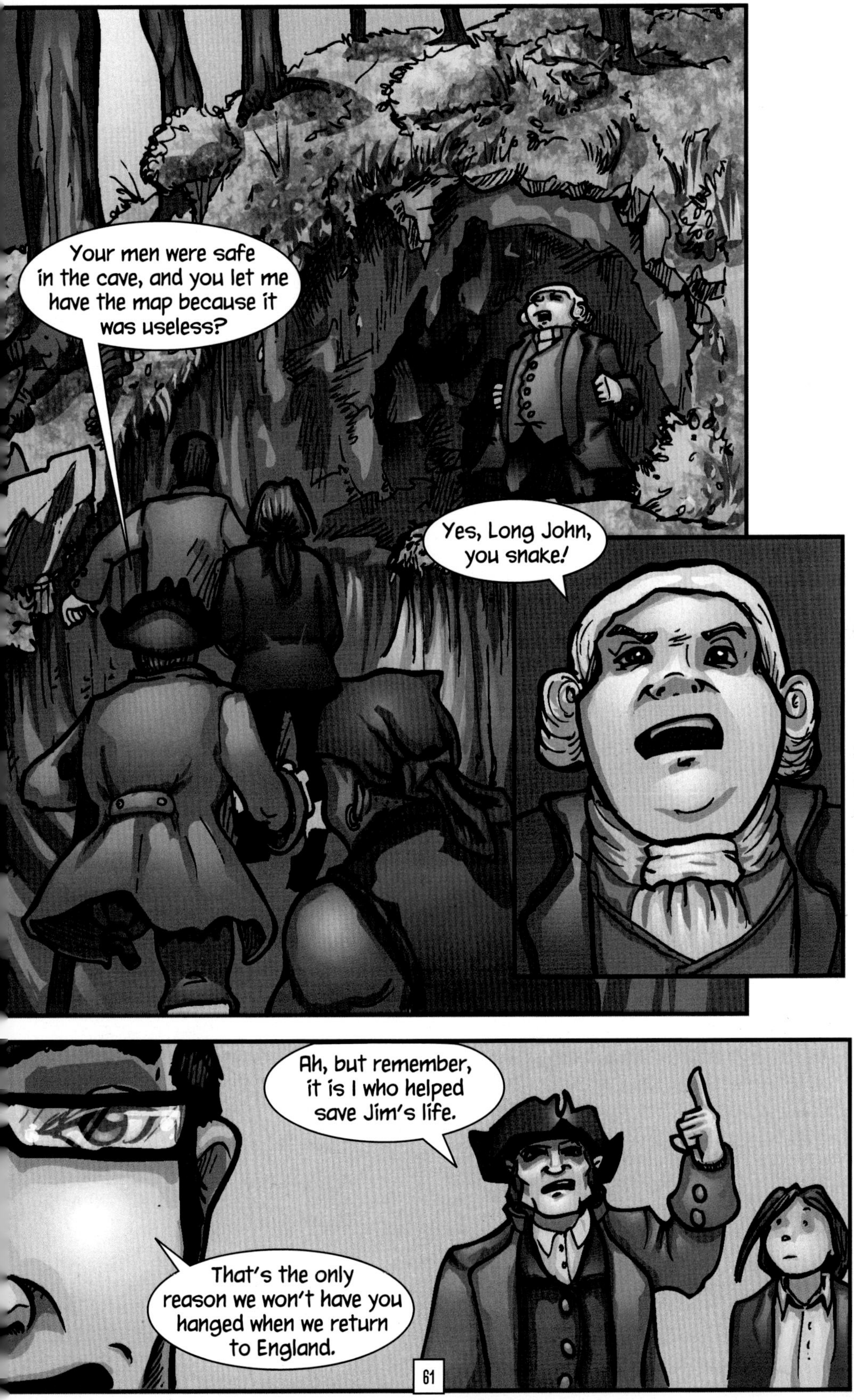

Your men were safe in the cave, and you let me have the map because it was useless?
Yes, Long John, you snake!
Ah, but remember, it is I who helped save Jim's life.
That's the only reason we won't have you hanged when we return to England.

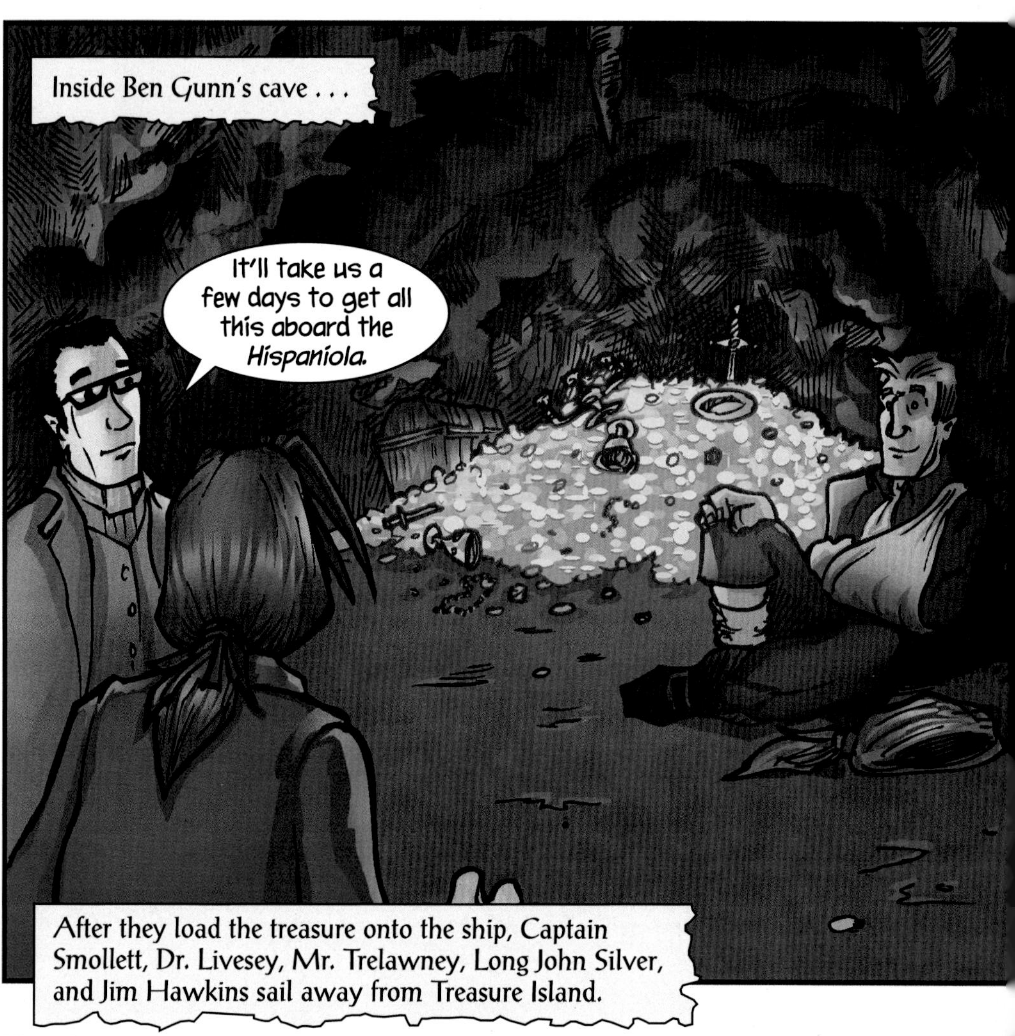
Inside Ben Gunn's cave . . .
It'll take us a few days to get all this aboard the *Hispaniola.*
After they load the treasure onto the ship, Captain Smollett, Dr. Livesey, Mr. Trelawney, Long John Silver, and Jim Hawkins sail away from Treasure Island.

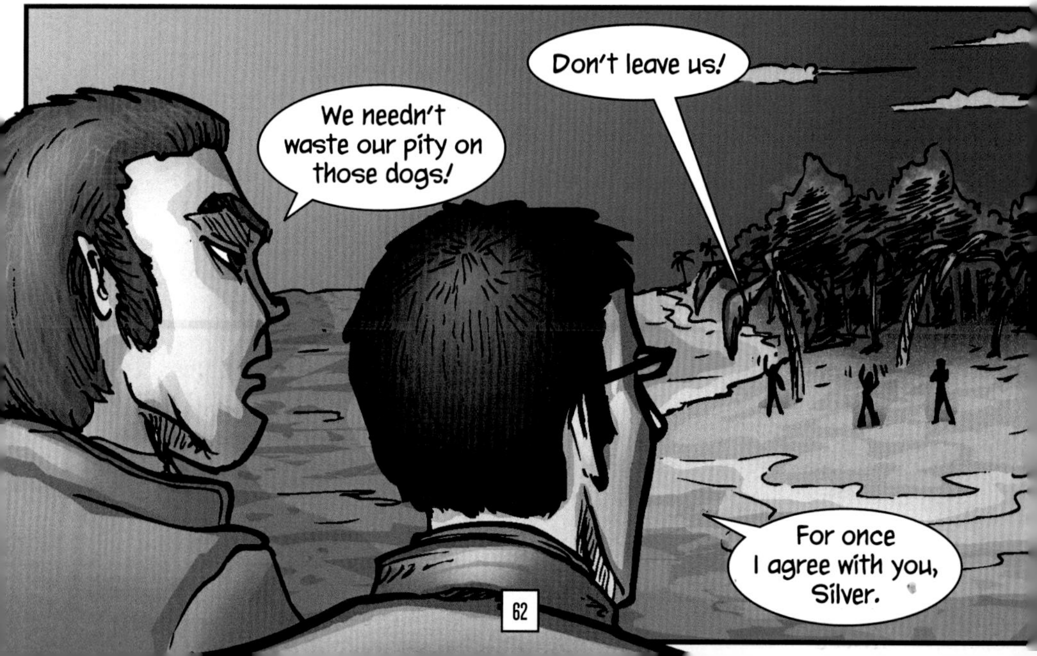
Don't leave us!
We needn't waste our pity on those dogs!
For once I agree with you, Silver.

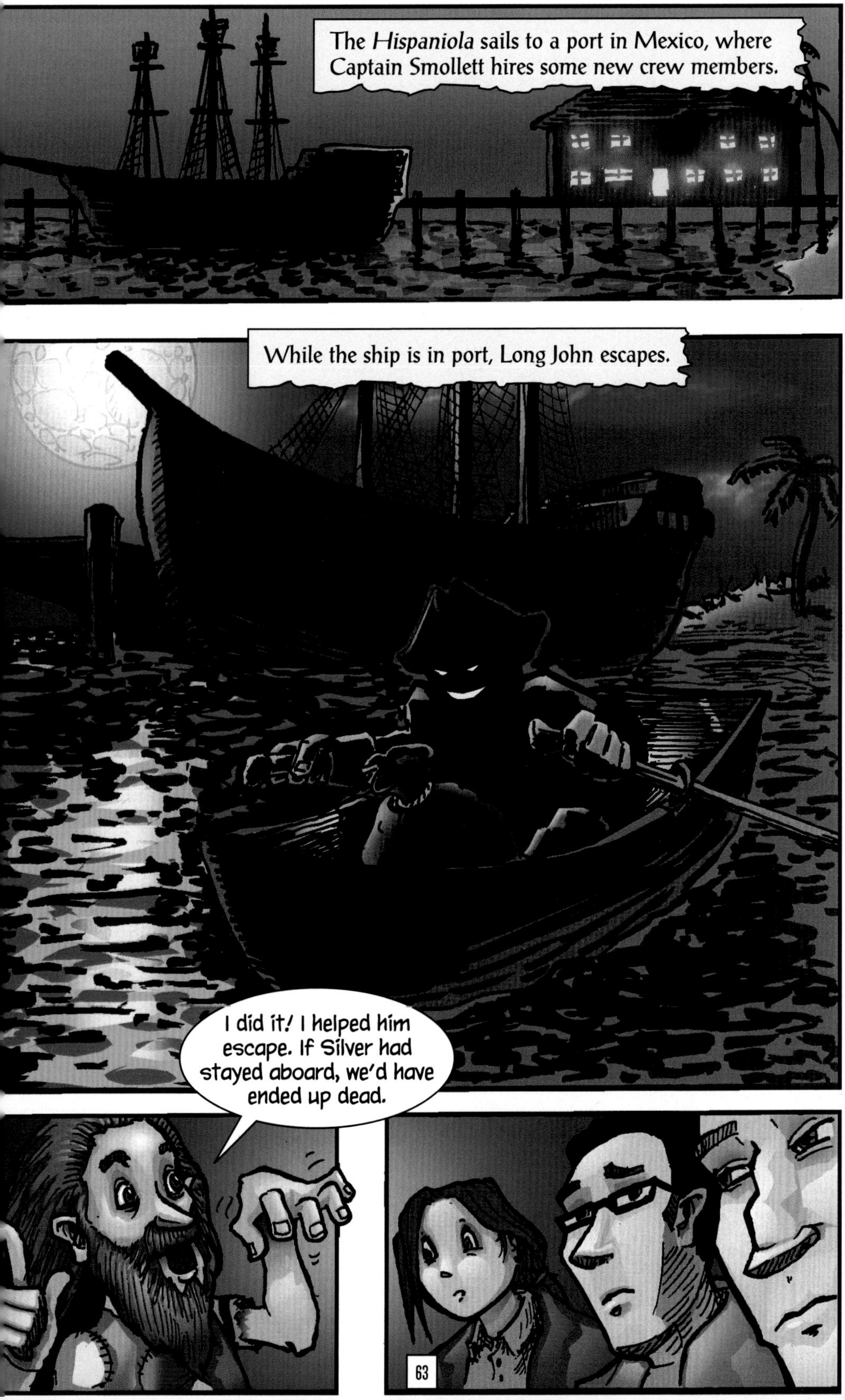
The *Hispaniola* sails to a port in Mexico, where Captain Smollett hires some new crew members.
While the ship is in port, Long John escapes.
I did it! I helped him escape. If Silver had stayed aboard, we'd have ended up dead.

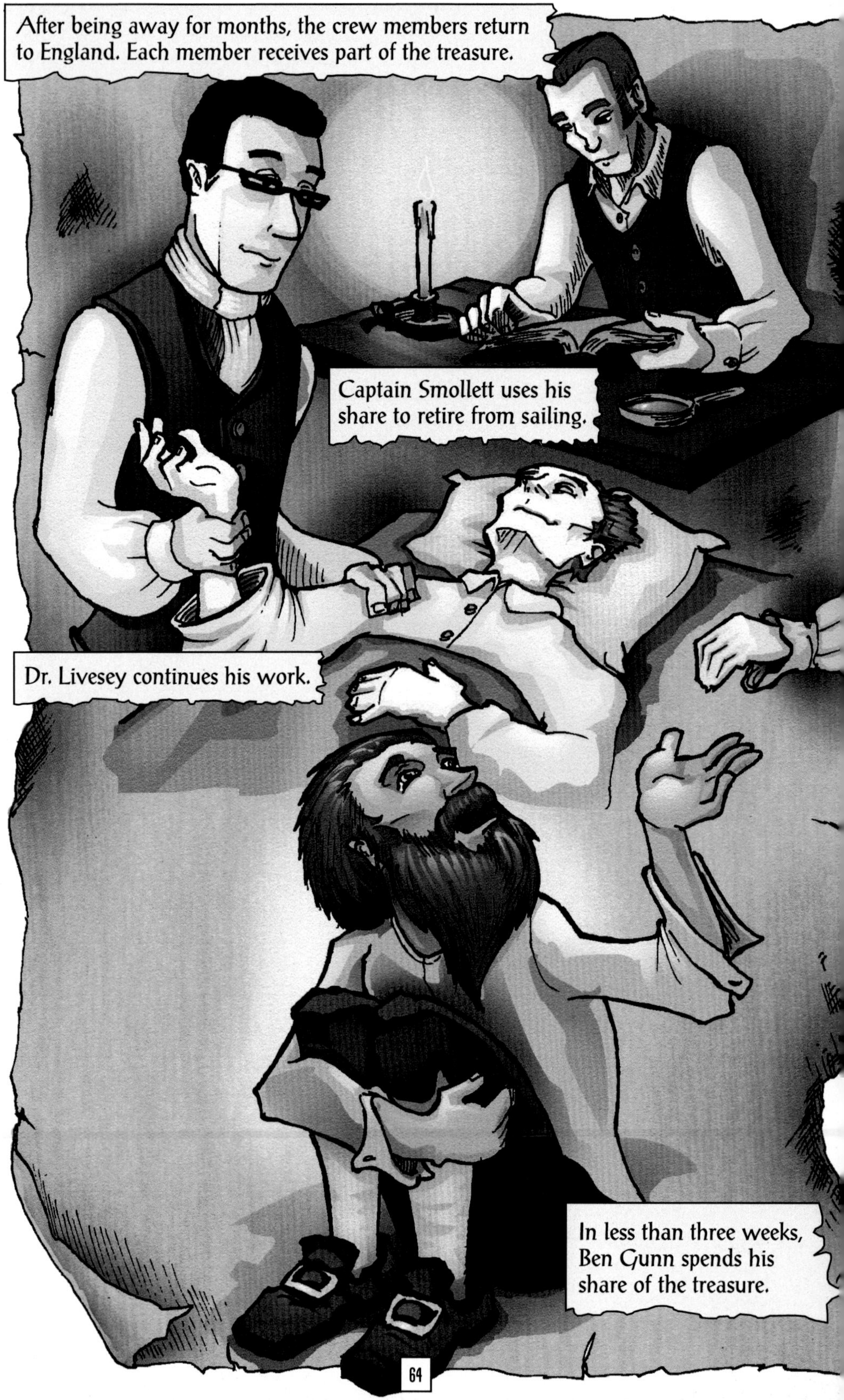
After being away for months, the crew members return to England. Each member receives part of the treasure.
Captain Smollett uses his share to retire from sailing.
Dr. Livesey continues his work.
In less than three weeks, Ben Gunn spends his share of the treasure.

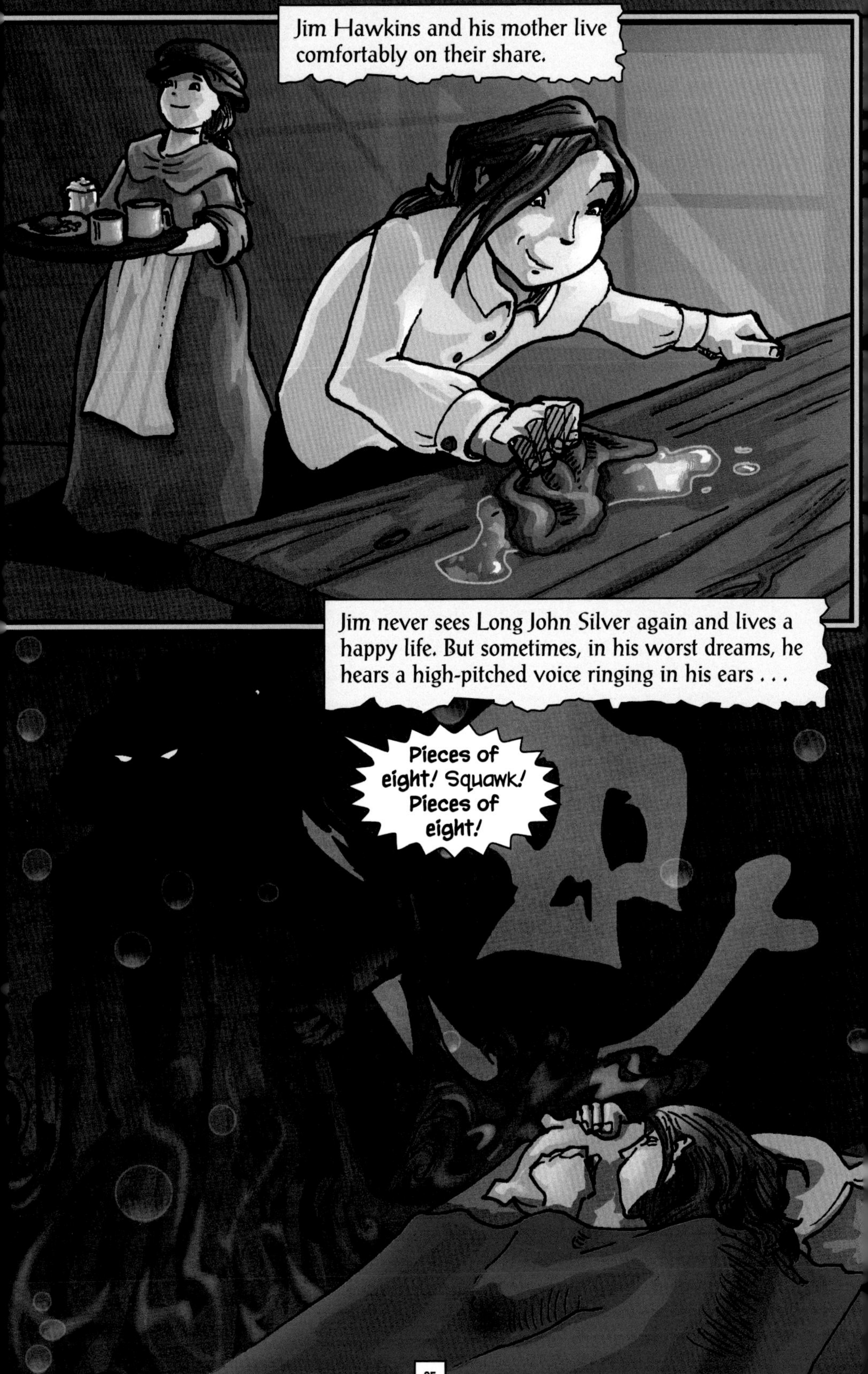
Jim Hawkins and his mother live comfortably on their share.
Jim never sees Long John Silver again and lives a happy life. But sometimes, in his worst dreams, he hears a high-pitched voice ringing in his ears . . .
Pieces of eight! Squawk! Pieces of eight!

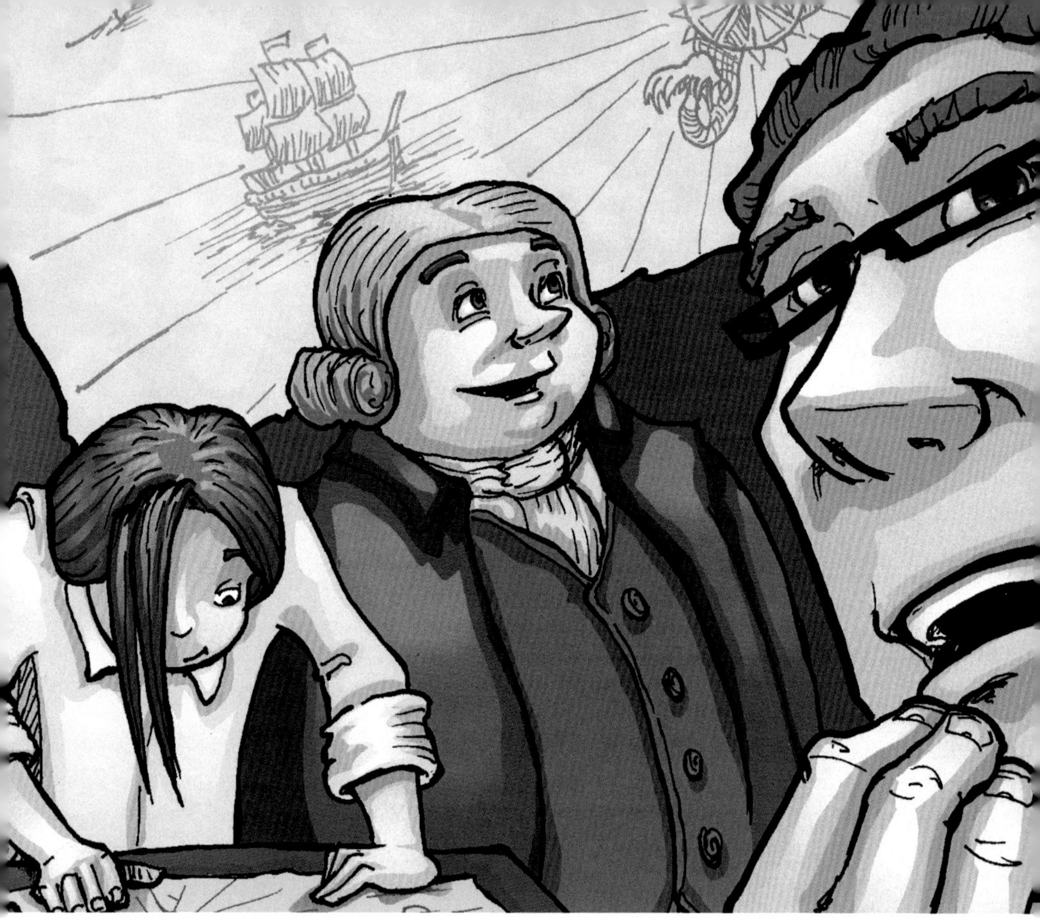

ABOUT THE RETELLING AUTHORS AND ILLUSTRATOR

Wim Coleman and **Pat Perrin** are a married couple who love writing books together. They have written many young adult nonfiction and fiction books, including retellings of classic novels, stories, and myths. They also run a scholarship program for Mexican students.

Greg Rebis was born in Queens, New York, but grew up mostly in central Florida. After working in civic government, pizza delivery, music retail and proofreading, he eventually landed work in publishing, film, and illustration. He loves art, sci-fi and video games.

GLOSSARY

ashore (uh-SHOR)—on or toward shore or land

beach (BEECH)—to land a ship on the shore

curiosity (kyur-ee-OSS-i-tee)—wanting to know more about things

inn (IN)—a small hotel, often with a restaurant

magistrate (MAJ-uh-strate)—a government official or judge who has the power to enforce the law

mate (MAYT)—a friend or person that someone works with

pieces of eight (PEESS-iz uhv ATE)—in pirate times, the Spanish currency was the peso, which was worth eight reales. Sometimes, a pirate would break the peso coin into eight pieces to make change.

seaman (SEE-man)—a sailor

shipwrecked (SHIP-rekt)—a ship that has been destroyed at sea

truce (TROOS)—an agreement to stop fighting

COMMON CORE ALIGNED
READING QUESTIONS

1. *Treasure Island* was initially published by chapters, one at a time. Readers sometimes waited over a week or more to receive the next section of the story. Do you think it might have been exciting to read this story one piece at a time? Why or why not? *("Refer to details and examples in a text when explaining what the text says.")*

2. Which character's point of view is most important in the story? What does he or she think about the events in the story? How do you know? *("Describe in depth a character, setting, or event in a story.")*

3. Action and adventure are both significant themes in *Treasure Island*. Can you find two examples of each? Make sure to note the page numbers for parts of the story you cite. *("Determine a theme of a story.")*

4. *Treasure Island* is famous for its settings and its characters' cool costumes. Choose one character and explain how their costumes are presented in the story. Then explain how it relates to the plot of the book. *("Describe in depth a character . . . drawing on specific details in the text.")*

5. At the end of the story, who receives the treasure's rewards? What do they do with their share of the riches? What would you do with your share of the riches? *("Refer to details and examples in a text when explaining what the text says explicitly and when drawing inferences from the text.")*

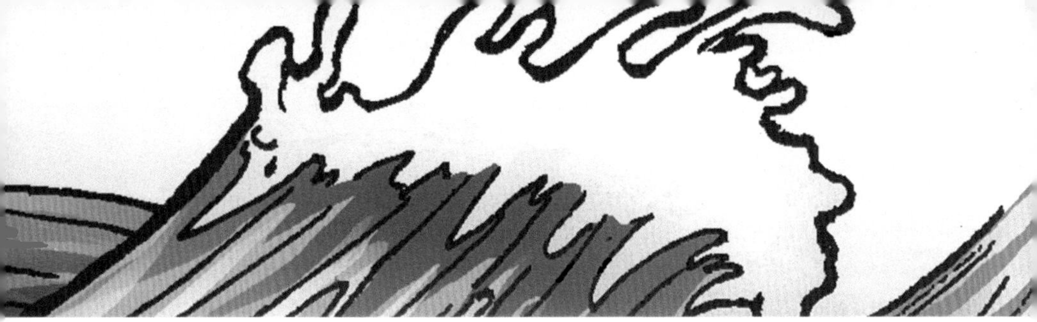

COMMON CORE ALIGNED

WRITING QUESTIONS

1. **Write a list of Jim Hawkin's job responsibilities at the beginning of the story. Then make another bulleted list of all the things Jim does to help his crew of friends by the end of the story. How did his responsibilities change as he gets older?** *("Draw evidence from literary . . . texts to support analysis.")*

2. **Picture Jim Hawkins waking up after a really vivid dream about his past adventure on Treasure Island. What kind of dream might he have? Write a dream journal entry from Jim Hawkins's perspective.** *("Write opinion pieces on topics or texts, supporting a point of view with reasons and information.")*

3. **Write an explanatory essay that outlines each step in this treasure hunting story. What happens at the beginning of the story? The middle? The end?** *("Write informative/explanatory texts to examine a topic and convey ideas.")*

4. **Imagine yourself as a character in the story. Who would you want to be? What would you look forward to doing in the story, and why?** *("Write narratives to develop real or imagined experiences or events.")*

5. **Describe Treasure Island. What does it look like? When you are done drawing evidence from the story to support your description, draw a picture of the island.** *("Draw evidence from literary . . . texts to support analysis.")*

READ THEM ALL!

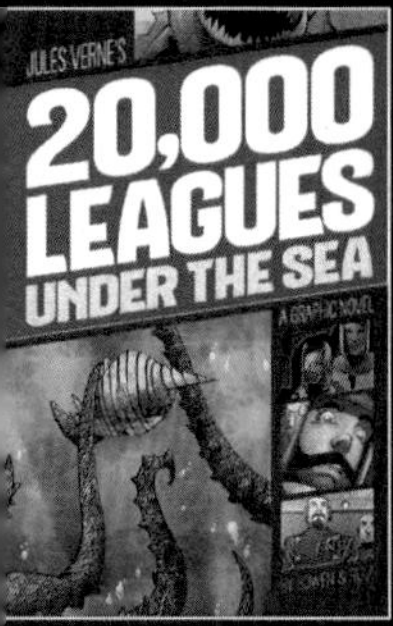
JULES VERNE'S
20,000 LEAGUES UNDER THE SEA
A GRAPHIC NOVEL

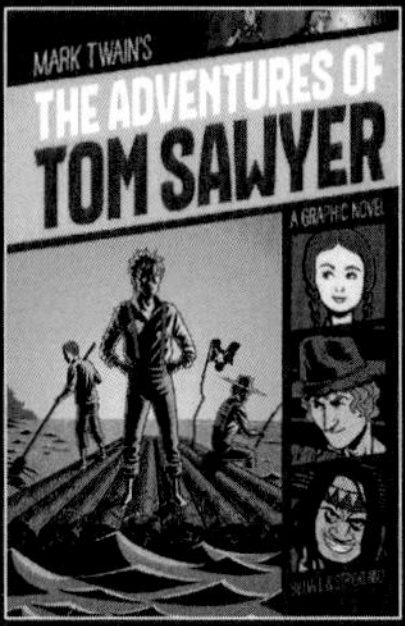
MARK TWAIN'S
THE ADVENTURES OF TOM SAWYER
A GRAPHIC NOVEL

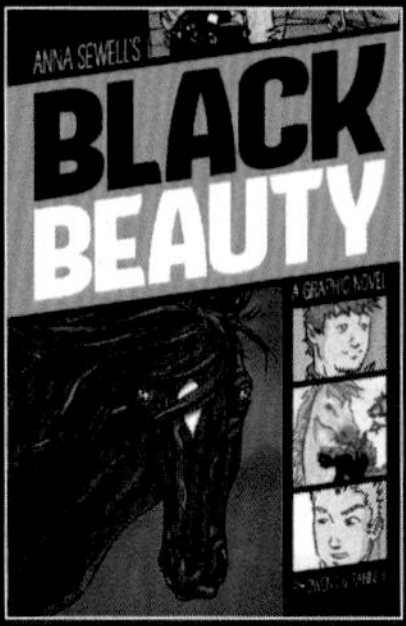
ANNA SEWELL'S
BLACK BEAUTY
A GRAPHIC NOVEL

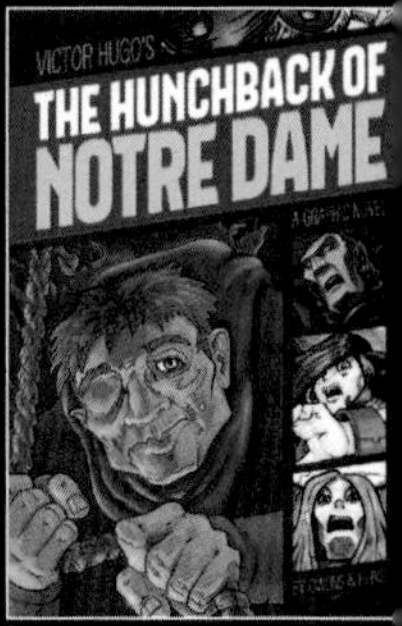
VICTOR HUGO'S
THE HUNCHBACK OF NOTRE DAME
A GRAPHIC NOVEL

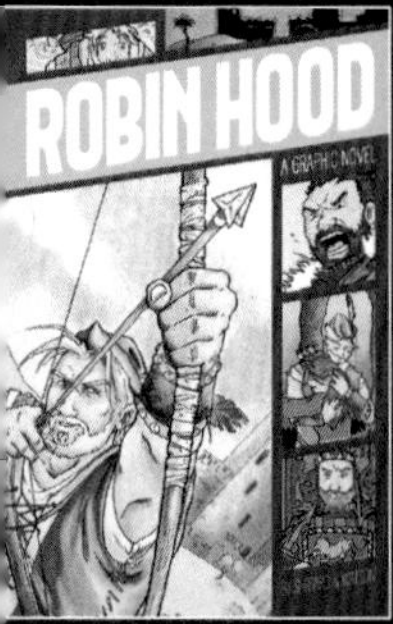
ROBIN HOOD
A GRAPHIC NOVEL

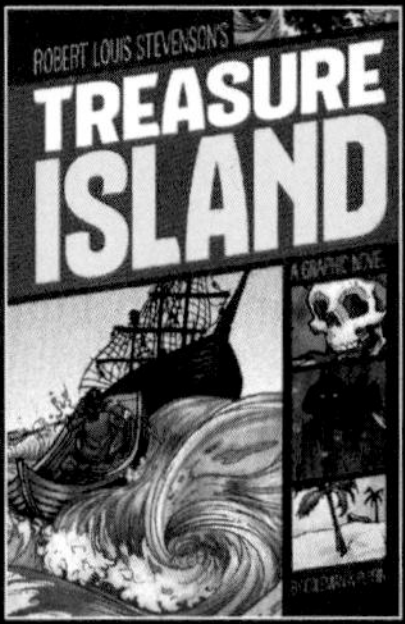
ROBERT LOUIS STEVENSON'S
TREASURE ISLAND
A GRAPHIC NOVEL

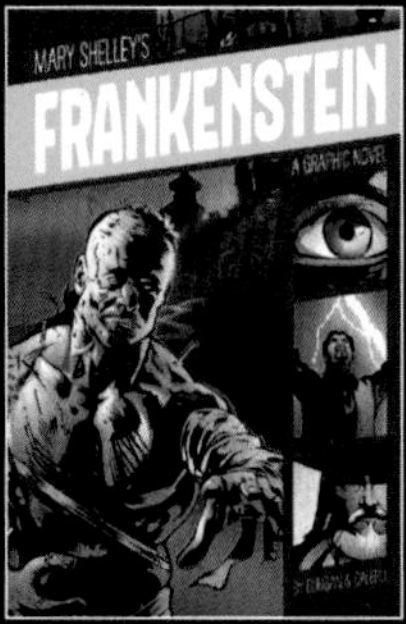
MARY SHELLEY'S
FRANKENSTEIN
A GRAPHIC NOVEL

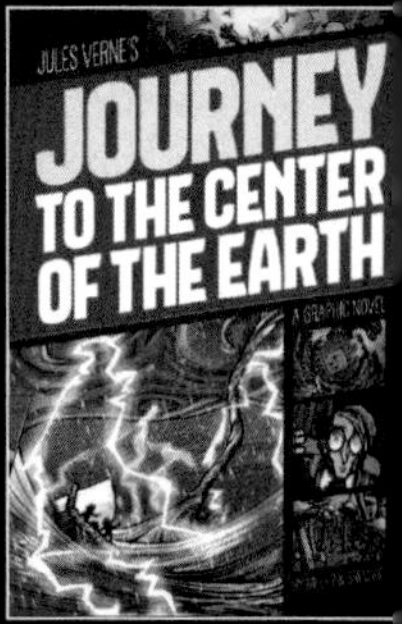
JULES VERNE'S
JOURNEY TO THE CENTER OF THE EARTH
A GRAPHIC NOVEL

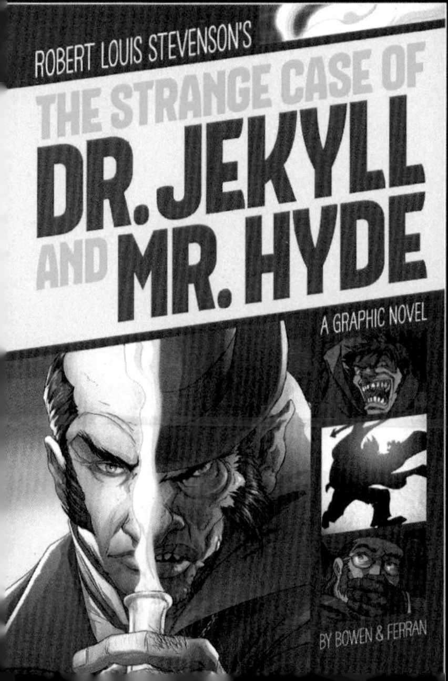
ROBERT LOUIS STEVENSON'S
THE STRANGE CASE OF DR. JEKYLL AND MR. HYDE
A GRAPHIC NOVEL
BY BOWEN & FERRAN

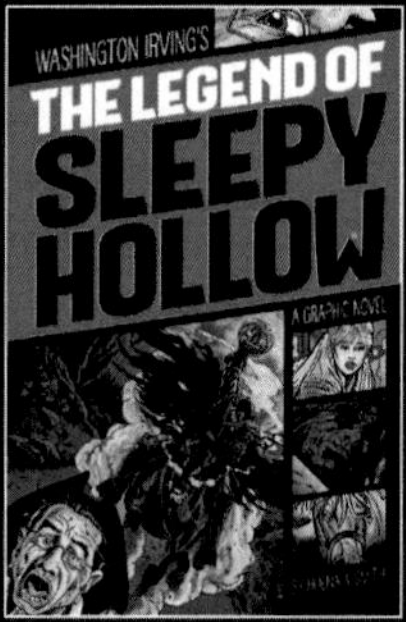
WASHINGTON IRVING'S
THE LEGEND OF SLEEPY HOLLOW
A GRAPHIC NOVEL

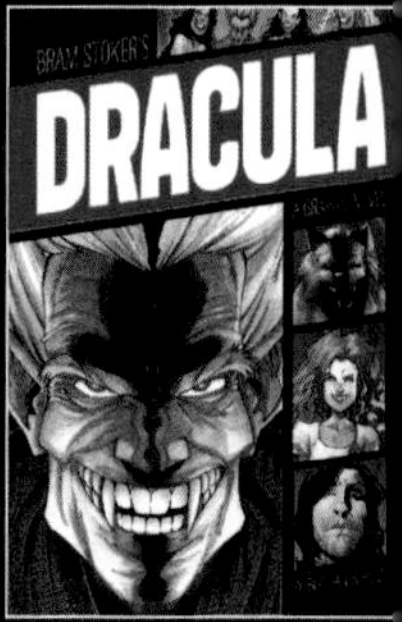
BRAM STOKER'S
DRACULA

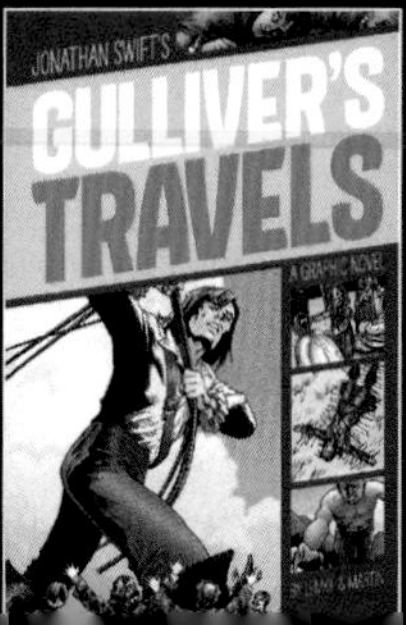
JONATHAN SWIFT'S
GULLIVER'S TRAVELS
A GRAPHIC NOVEL

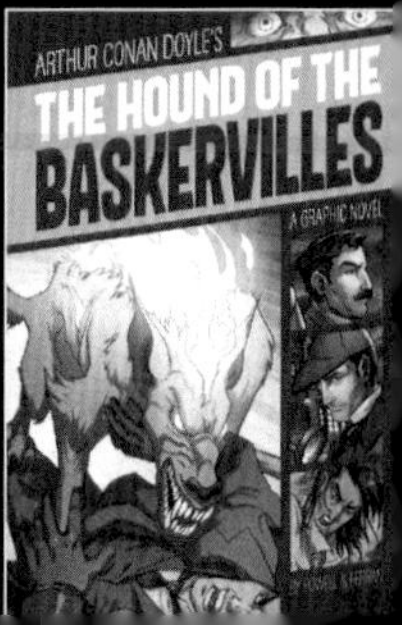
ARTHUR CONAN DOYLE'S
THE HOUND OF THE BASKERVILLES
A GRAPHIC NOVEL

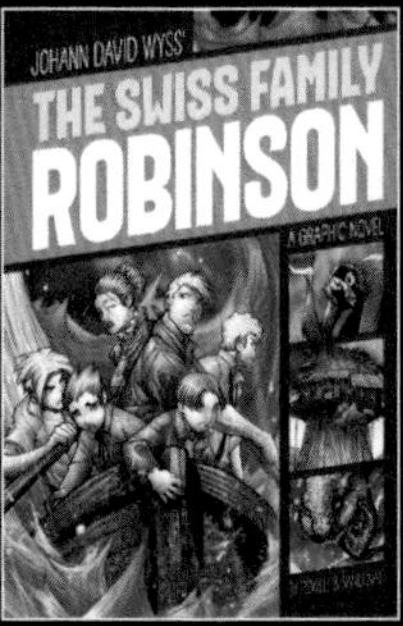
JOHANN DAVID WYSS'
THE SWISS FAMILY
ROBINSON
A GRAPHIC NOVEL

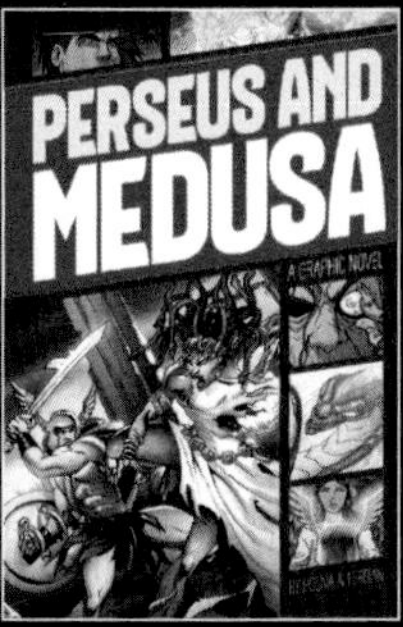
PERSEUS AND
MEDUSA
A GRAPHIC NOVEL

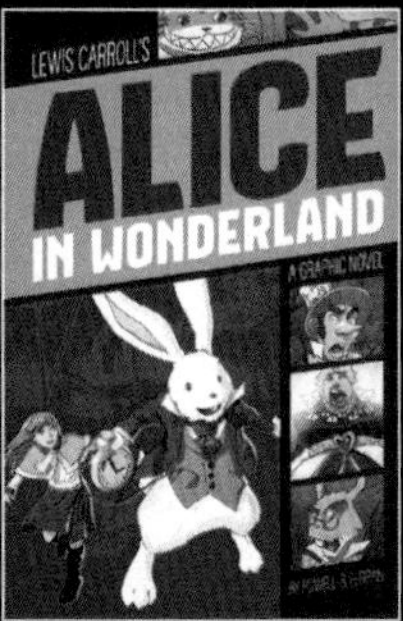
LEWIS CARROLL'S
ALICE
IN WONDERLAND
A GRAPHIC NOVEL

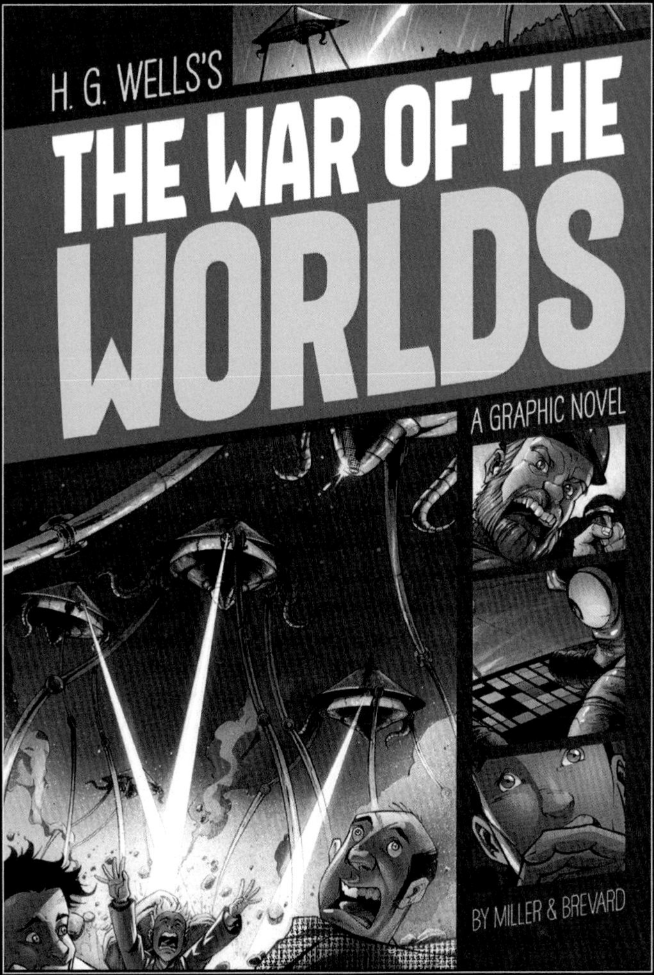
H. G. WELLS'S
THE WAR OF THE
WORLDS
A GRAPHIC NOVEL
BY MILLER & BREVARD

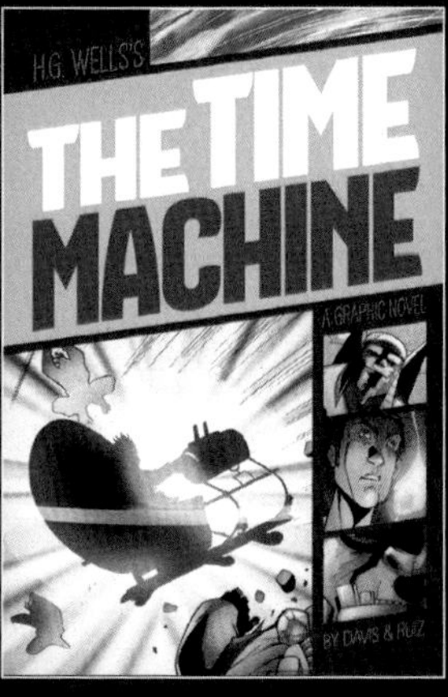
H.G. WELLS'S
THE TIME
MACHINE
A GRAPHIC NOVEL
BY DAVIS & RUIZ

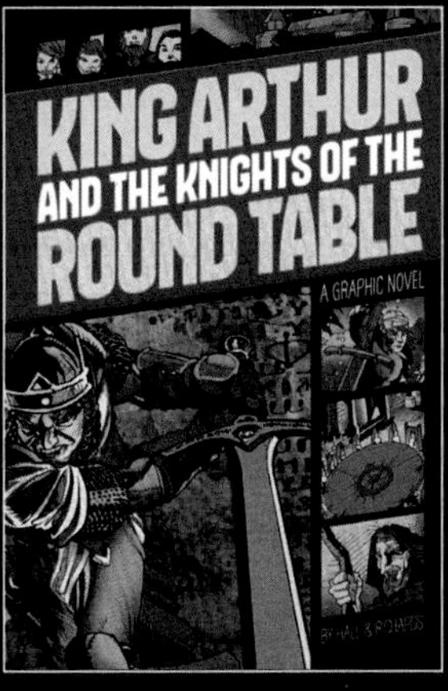
KING ARTHUR
AND THE KNIGHTS OF THE
ROUND TABLE
A GRAPHIC NOVEL

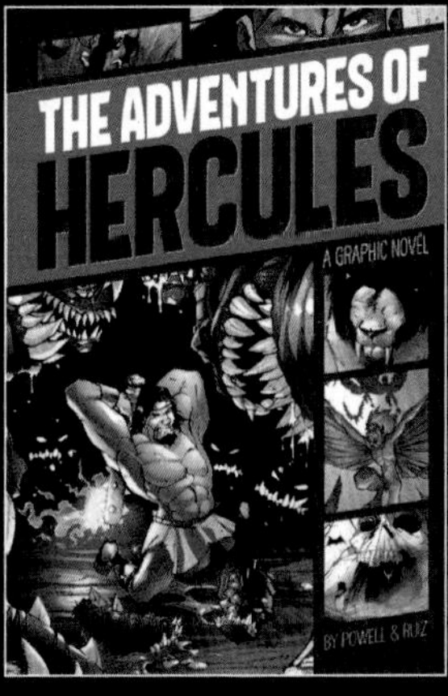
THE ADVENTURES OF
HERCULES
A GRAPHIC NOVEL
BY POWELL & RUIZ